Dark Corner

A Witch Cat Mystery Book 2

VICKI VASS

*To Charlotte for providing insight
into my new adopted home and its environs.*

ACKNOWLEDGMENTS

THANKS TO D.A. SARAC FOR her professional editing and enthusiasm for Asheville, Tracker, who is turning into a great dog, Terra and most importantly, the real Pixel.

October 31, 1862
Black Mountain, North Carolina

"TERRA, RUN NOW. THEY'RE COMING." Agatha's words echoed across the open field. I glanced up at her. I lay in the crop field that Agatha had been tending. We were at the top of a clearing outside her cabin on Black Mountain, part of the Blue Ridge Mountains in Western North Carolina. I stared deep into her turquoise eyes. I saw fear rising up from her. She stood, putting a hand to her lower back, and stared across the field. The purple flowers of the chives rustled in the breeze; the evergreens that surrounded her land swayed in the wind. Her red and white dogs sensed the intruders approaching. They darted around the field, barking, circling her, ready to protect her from whatever evil approached.

"Go, Terra, before it's too late." Her voice was more urgent this time.

I stood and stretched, realizing I couldn't remember when she had become so old, her hair gray, her skin withered and wrinkled, her movements slow and unsure. I was reluctant to leave her. Since arriving in North Carolina, Agatha had provided me with refuge, allowing me to curl up by her fire, eat from her table, and accompany her on healing ministries. A woman of few words, she was a powerful healer. Despite her abilities, she still had not found a way to heal me. I remained as a cat, my true girl form hidden from me. At seventeen years of age, escaping from the trials in Salem, I took a potion that transformed me into an ordinary alley cat, and thus I have stayed. The knowledge to change me back to my true form was lost with my coven leader, Elizabeth, who had met her fate in the Salem witch trials.

I felt the pounding of the hooves charging across the field and the rattle of the heavy wagon before I saw them. Then I heard the telltale rebel yell. Garbed in yellow and gray, there were three men, two on horseback, brandishing pistols and one, the leader, driving a horse-drawn wagon. They stopped in front of Agatha, who was as surprised as I was. No intruders had ever broken through the enchanted woods around the cabin. The dogs barked, circling the wagon. Two black horses frothed at the mouth and kicked up their hooves. The wheels of the wagon sunk deep into the ground. Like the horses, the wagon was black. Holding the reins was a lieutenant, tall and thin. He cracked his whip as he stared the dogs down. The dogs whimpered and stepped backward. The oldest dog lunged toward him, and the whip cracked again. I ran and hid behind the wagon. Dangling from the bed hung bones tied with tendons. One sniff and I could tell they were human. Trophies, I thought, spoils of this brutal war.

As the dogs continued to lunge and bark, he cracked his whip toward them.

"No," Agatha screamed, standing in front of the dog. "Run," she screamed at her dogs as the whip cracked, lashing the flesh off her arm, causing her to drop to her knees.

Snarling, the largest dog lunged for the lieutenant, attempting to pull him down from the wagon. The whip cracked again, wrapping around the dog's neck. The lieutenant pulled the whip, snapping the poor dog's neck. The other pups scattered. Clutching her arm, Agatha knelt down next to the dog, cradling his head in her lap.

I stopped, stepped toward her, and then froze in place when I saw the face of the lieutenant. His face was scarred, his mouth distorted with a comical grin that stretched ear to ear. What kind of battle had he been through? He tugged at the kerchief around his neck, revealing the deep red scar that hung like a noose around it.

I ran into the fields toward the stream, the dogs behind me. We scattered, the dogs making their way into the stream, me avoiding water. The soldiers had been targeting Agatha since the conflict started as she would not declare a loyalty to either side. Blue or gray, she treated both with her healing medications. Agatha was not a proponent of war. Nor was I. I had lost too many friends to conflicts. I leaned against a mighty oak, catching my breath. I clawed my way up the tree, finding comfort on a heavy limb. From my vantage point, I watched as the lieutenant dismounted and circled Agatha. There was something about him, the lieutenant, that chilled me to the bone. His eyes stared past Agatha as though he could see through her. I had seen other soldiers, some mere boys, others old men. The lieutenant was neither. I looked at him, yet I didn't see him. It was moments ago, yet I couldn't remember his face, any of his features except the lieutenant bars on his uniform and the cracking of his whip.

They came without warning. Agatha Hollows enchanted the cabin and the woods surrounding it. The ash, oak, and thorn bent their mighty limbs over the road leading up Black Mountain, barring the way to any unwanted strangers. I had not heard them crack, and I had never seen Agatha Hollows truly scared. My heart pounded. The war was coming to Black Mountain; the war was coming to Agatha Hollows.

FAREWELL TO EMMA TANGLEDWOOD

Present Day, Black Mountain, North Carolina

I GAZED ACROSS THE OPEN FIELD surrounding the cabin, Agatha Hollows's cabin up Black Mountain, North Carolina. For the most part, it stood well, being two hundred years old. The covered front porch had its share of creaking boards but still was a comfortable place to rock. We had patched the roof and replaced the front steps. Besides that, the cabin stood as it did when Agatha Hollows stood in it.

Eighteen-year-old Abigail lay on the ground, a book of Appalachian folk remedies open in front of her. Her long hair, once blond, now almost white since her turning into a full-blooded witch. Her skin was iridescent, but the most remarkable change were her eyes from sky blue to violet, the same color as her great-grandmother's eyes—the sign of a very powerful witch. The humans call it albinism, a condition caused by a lack of pigment in skin, hair, and eyes. Light passes through the eyes and reflects back out, causing the irises to appear violet. In the case of Abigail, her change was not from lack of pigment but the opposite. She had become a perfect being, able to see all the colors of the human and witch spectrum. As her powers grew, she would also be able to see the colors of the alternate realms. For now, she appeared to be merely an amazingly beautiful young woman. Her Australian shepherd puppy, Tracker, shared her eye color as familiars do. Abigail was able to see through Tracker's eyes. Ghost eyes is what the Native Americans called them, considering these puppies sacred.

If I were still a girl in my former body, I would be jealous of her, but I was trapped in this feline body, elegant and slender but a cat just the same. Heads turned when Abigail walked, her elfin body glided, slicing through the air. I asked her repeatedly to dress more ladylike, a remnant of my upbringing. She refused, donning her ripped jeans and leather jacket. Even in peasant garb, she carried the air of royalty as well she should as she was the heir to the throne of the Oakhavens. Great-granddaughter of Elizabeth Oakhaven, Abigail was the keeper of the Oakhaven bloodline, descendants of the original earth walkers, white witches with unlimited power. I loved Abigail as I loved Elizabeth. For that reason, I devoted my life to training and protecting her. Unfortunately, she shared her great-grandmother's stubborn streak. I found my patience growing short with her.

I heard gurgling noises and turned to see Tracker carrying a protesting fluffy orange tabby in his mouth. He prefers me to describe him as fluffy, not chubby, Pixel he does. Since the recent darkness had ebbed, the Australian shepherd pup had resorted to puppy behavior, and taunting Pixel was his favorite play. "No, Tracker," I scolded him, but he did not understand or chose not to. He continued nipping at Pixel and taunting him.

My protests drew Abigail's attention from her book. "Tracker, put Pixel down." The puppy obeyed and ran to Abigail's side, wiggling his tailless butt.

Pixel dusted off his fur. He stood upright and pranced away. "Me hungry," I heard him say as he made his way toward the stream, which flowed adjacent to the cabin.

I could follow him, search for food, but I was uneasy leaving Abigail. I felt a stirring in the air. It brought back memories of intruders descending upon Agatha Hollows so long ago. Chills traveled through my fur. Pixel flew back as though he felt my fear. He tilted his head and then pounced on me.

"Pixel, we're fine. Nothing to worry about," I told him.

Pixel gave me another sideways glance. He sensed when I was telling half-truths. Not that I would lie to him, but I thought it best at times to conceal the complete truth from him.

"Terra, why won't you let me read my great-grandmother's book of spells?" Abigail slammed the book she was reading shut, not the one she was referring to.

"You're not ready for the power contained in that book yet, Abigail. You have to understand who you are first before you become who you should be. Your magic is entwined with these woods just as Agatha Hollows was, that's why I have you studying the Appalachian folklore."

"I thought my family was from Salem."

"Yes, that's true, Abigail, but before that from Ireland. And before Ireland, they were." I stopped myself. "That's something we'll talk about once you are able to understand." I stepped across the book, rubbing my body across Abigail's face. Abigail ran her fingers along my fur until our attention was drawn away by Pixel.

My friend, the big orange cat, scampered about, trying to catch the first dragonfly of spring. He stopped suddenly, stuck his nose up in the air, and the dragonfly landed on his head. He crossed his eyes, trying to see it, and then he let out a Pixel roar of laughter. The dragonfly flew off with Pixel in pursuit.

"You always say I'm never ready. I've read every book you've given me. I know how to make a mustard plaster, insect repellents, and even a love potion. I think I can even churn butter if I had to, so what's the point, Terra?" Abigail reached into the pocket of her leather jacket and pulled out a cigarette.

I jumped on her lap, swatting it out of her hand.

"Hey," she yelled, pushing me off her lap.

I landed in a mud puddle, then jumped out. The mud clung to me.

Abigail put her hand over her mouth to hold back her laughter. "Gee, really, really sorry," she said, not attempting to conceal her sarcasm or her laughter.

I shook myself off. I had reached my limit. "Are you done, Abigail? Did you enjoy that?"

"Geez, Terra, it was an accident, okay?"

"I told you I don't want you smoking. It will kill you."

"So I survived the tornado of black magic, but one cigarette is going to kill me. I don't think so." She reached in her pocket and pulled out another cigarette.

"Okay, Abigail, put away the cigarette. It's time," I said.

She paused with the cigarette halfway up to her lips, the lighter half-open in her other hand. "Time for what?"

"Go get the broom on the front porch."

Abigail ran up the steps and brought back the old straw broom leaning against the rocking chair. "What's this for?"

"I think it's time you learned to fly."

"But you said that the whole flying broom thing was a myth. That's not how witches fly."

"I said that because you weren't ready and I didn't want you running off and trying to ride your first broom and crashing."

"Really, Terra? I'm going to fly."

"Yes," I told her.

"Okay, what do I do?" She held the broom.

"First you need to straddle the broom."

"Okay." Abigail did.

I went up the front stairs, jumped on the railing for a good vantage point. Pixel bounded back and joined me on the railing. "What doing?" Pixel said.

"I'm having fun with Abigail."

"Me like fun."

"Okay, Abigail, now you need to get a good running start."

Abigail ran across the length of the front of the house and then back and then again and then again. "Nothing's happening," she yelled.

"You have to create enough lift. The faster you run, the more lift you'll create."

"Okay," she said, panting.

Pixel gazed at me. "We're playing a joke on Abigail," I said.

Pixel roared and fell off the railing. He jumped back up.

"Wait, wait, Abigail," I said.

Abigail stopped, huffing and puffing, clutching the broom.

"You have to recite the flight incantation while you're running."

"Now you tell me," Abigail said. "Okay, fine, what is it?"

"It's Ohwhatas, illygoo, siam."

Abigail began running with the broom between her legs, shouting, "Ohwhatas, illygoo, siam."

"Faster, Abigail," I yelled.

Back and forth she ran. "Ohwhatas, illygoo, siam."

"Say the words faster."

"Ohwhatasill—" Abigail stopped dead and then said, "Oh, what a silly goose I am."

Pixel fell off the railing again. Abigail snapped the broom in two over her knee and stormed into the house.

Pixel inhaled deeply. "Me hungry?" He could smell what I did—Mrs. Twiggs's cauldron boiling with a concoction for which I had given her the recipe. He scurried into the cabin with Tracker and me close behind.

"Oh dear, Terra, I don't think I'm doing this right." The new Mrs. Twiggs, light on her feet Mrs. Twiggs, filled her wooden ladle from the iron cauldron hanging above the fire in the big stone fireplace and breathed in. Since her transformation to a Wiccan, Mrs. Twiggs had turned into a much younger woman. Not so much that the humans could tell but enough that those close to her could. "I followed every step in Agatha's recipe. I know I did." She shook her head.

Pixel tiptoed up to the cauldron, stood on his hind paws, and sniffed. "Me like." He grinned at me, his smile resembling that of the Cheshire cat from *Alice in Wonderland*. Pixel's days were full of new discoveries, and his delight in them never ceased to delight me.

Over the past few months, Mrs. Twiggs had spent most of her time at the cabin, helping me with Abigail's schooling. She understood we needed Abigail to become who she was meant to be—a powerful witch in a long line of powerful witches. The Leaf & Page, her cozy tea and vintage bookshop in downtown Biltmore Village, had been shuttered. She felt it best left in the good hands of her deceased, beloved husband, Albert.

"It takes time, Mrs. Twiggs. Magic is a study of patience and repetition. Just the slightest wrong turn of the spoon or a pinch too much of this or that and any potion can turn bad." I said with authority. I had learned this firsthand from Elizabeth, who

I studied under in Salem. "All magic is chemistry. The chemistry of combining herbs and ingredients but also the chemistry of the witch who brews them."

"I don't know why this isn't working, Terra. You said Agatha used this potion to bring on visions."

As Mrs. Twiggs talked, Pixel leaped up and reached with his paw to bring the spoon to his mouth. He lapped the potion up before we could stop him. "Mmm, good. Pixel like. Pixel like." I knocked the spoon away from him. He stopped in his tracks, shaking his tail ferociously. His eyes dilated. "Feel funny, Terra. Pixel feel funny. Pixel no like." Pixel's eyes rolled back into his head. He whispered in my ear, "They come. The hunters come." His eyes rolled back, and he pounced on me. "Me hungry. Me hungry."

"What just happened?" Mrs. Twiggs asked. "I tried the potion and had no visions."

I had no response. Pixel was an ordinary cat—no, I do him injustice, he's an extraordinary cat, fearless and brave but a cat all the same.

Mrs. Twiggs scooped the ladle again and brought it down so I could lap from it. The potion tasted gritty against my tongue. I waited for the explosion of light but nothing. I didn't have any traces of the gift of vision. I never had even when I was a girl. Mrs. Twiggs on the other hand didn't need any potion to peer into the future. Her gifts included prophecy, but we had yet to determine her Wiccan ancestry. I had her make the recipe, hoping her bloodline would be revealed.

Abigail sulked in the corner, guitar in her hand.

"I have dinner on the stove," Mrs. Twiggs said.

We all sat down at the small kitchen table. Mrs. Twiggs served up the honey ham, sweet potatoes, and fresh biscuits. Pixel gobbled his up, making slurping noises. I ate more slowly, skipping the potatoes.

"Terra, I've invited the ladies over. They are still recovering from the events of Halloween, and I think we need to ease their minds." Mrs. Twiggs referred to the Ladies of the Biltmore Society, our local group of Wiccans. Before transforming into their true Wiccan selves, the ladies had been a garden club devoted to maintaining the legacy of Frederick Law Olmsted, the master gardener who created the gardens at the Biltmore Estate. The ladies had recently defeated a darkness that had settled over Asheville, the town nestled in the Blue Ridge Mountains where we had made our home.

"It's because of those events that we need to continue their training," I said.

"I thought that was all over. That we're safe now," Abigail said.

I didn't want to let the others know yet that we'll never be truly safe. The magic we had woken in Asheville was a beacon shining out to the rest of the world and beyond. Creatures following that beacon would come. I hoped that Mrs. Twiggs's powers or a premonition enhanced by Agatha Hollows's potion would give us sufficient warning to prepare for the battle to come. "We must always be ready and keep our skills sharp, Abigail. For now, let us enjoy our meal."

Tracker sat patiently by Abigail's side. He was now a full-grown dog, nearly sixty pounds. He waited on any movement of her hand signaling treats from the table. Pixel had finished and was now hovering over Mrs. Twiggs, purring and nudging against her, seeking seconds and thirds.

I finished my meal with relish, washing it down with the saucer of cream Mrs. Twiggs shared with Pixel and me.

"I'll clear the table. We'll have dessert when the ladies come. I've made peach tarts." Mrs. Twiggs bustled around the table, clearing the dishes, humming softly to herself.

Abigail sat by the fire, strumming her guitar. It was her most prized possession. I leaped onto the stool next to her. "Terra, why am I wasting my time with these spell books? I've read everything you've given me, memorized every potion, every incantation."

"You're not ready for your great-grandmother's book."

"You told me I'm the only one who can wield it. I'm not afraid of it."

"Because you're not afraid that means you're not ready to open it." Abigail and I had this argument constantly.

"All these spells you have me practicing are useless. This spell right here." Abigail reached down and picked up a book called *Spellbound*. She read out loud. "Tied by knots of thread, held by hands of dead, bound by earth, covered by dirt, lie eternal by woods."

I knew that spell well. Agatha had used it often with the folk who lived in the nearby cabins. "Appalachians believe the dead would come back to life if not put to rest. Agatha used that spell not only to calm their fears but as a precaution against dark spirits that preyed on the newly dead."

"Did it work?"

"Not really."

"Why am I practicing it?"

"Because Agatha believed it would work. While the occasion never arose that a dark spirit brought a body back to life doesn't mean it couldn't happen. More importantly, you have to understand the history of the power you wield. Your family oak is the center of that power, and like the rings of its trunk that power radiates throughout these Western North Carolina woods. Agatha's magic was also part of these woods, so understand your history first."

Abigail shut the book with a snap and put it down. She went back to her guitar. She did not have the patience yet for what I needed to teach her. And I did not have the experience to be a teacher. I was Elizabeth's apprentice; Abigail's great-grandmother had been my mentor. I felt a bit of a fraud trying to teach magic to a witch who would grow to be more powerful than I would ever be.

"They here. They here," Pixel singsonged from his perch on the windowsill. I glanced out the window and saw the cars pulling up to the cabin. The ladies were here, all of them wearing their black ceremonial cloaks and pointed hats. The hats were not necessary, but the ladies insisted on wearing them. One by one, they filed up the cabin steps. Doris Stickman first, tall and thin as a rail, her ebony skin glistening in the moonlight. She was followed by the much smaller Nupur Bartlett, her red Bindi on her forehead representing her strength. The smallest of all the ladies, she was our most powerful warrior. Next came the wide Jean Branchworthy, with her moon-pie face. She stopped and smiled at me with her smoky eyes. Then Gwendolyn Birchbark, who stopped and politely bowed, a dichotomy of her proper Chinese heritage and her Southern warmth and hospitality. Following her was the freckle-faced Caroline Bowers. I bowed politely. Her bloodline was royal, dating back to Rhiannon the queen of witches. In the previous weeks, she had been conversing with me in my dreams. Wanda Raintree almost skipped up the steps, her hair tied in a single braid, wrapped in Cherokee turquoise and silver. Then the youngest of them all, June Loblolly, our Viking princess. She carried her hat, her hair flowed free, a silver carved circlet on the crown of her head. She walked with poise, demonstrating her former modeling career. Since turning, all the ladies walked purposely in contrast to their outward human appearance of old age. These ladies were our coven.

"Terra, dear, can you come over tomorrow? I want to practice my magic but find I need your help to do it," Jean Branchworthy said to me as she continuously snapped her fingers trying to exude a spark. "See. Nothing."

I nodded as the ladies settled down, each taking a seat around the table. Pixel pranced around their feet, tail upright, sniffing for any hidden treat and making gurgling noises.

Mrs. Twiggs slowly walked to the table, carrying a very old and tattered black pointed witch's hat. She carefully and respectfully placed it in the center of the table. All the ladies removed their hats and placed them in a circle around the hat.

"Tonight, we remember our fallen sister, Emma Tangledwood. We pray for her light to follow its true path to the next world while we release her magic into our world." Each of the ladies stood and placed a hand on Mrs. Tangledwood's hat. The ceremony was a token of love, grief, and respect.

I drifted away, remembering a similar night. A group of young Cherokee healers had come to train with Agatha. She closed the curtains as the candle glow illuminated her long, angular face. I saw a glimpse of her true self, and I never looked at her the same way again. My eyes flew open. I thought I saw Mrs. Tangledwood's hat move, just a twitch, no more than a field mouse's whisker. I rubbed my eyes in disbelief until I noticed the ladies appeared to have seen it also. They were quiet, wide-eyed, and waiting. Another twitch. A collective gasp rose from the ladies gathered around the table. This was not Emma Tangledwood; this was not of her making. The hat flew off the table, knocking Mrs. Stickman to the ground.

"Abigail," I shouted. "Read the incantation—now—Abigail, speak the words," I urged her, rubbing against her with force.

Abigail stood, watching the hat in disbelief as it flung into dishes and crashed into pots and pans.

Mrs. Loblolly grabbed the hat in midair and wrestled it to the floor, wrapping her body over it. When she looked up to smile at us, she was hurled into the blazing fireplace.

Mrs. Stickman raised her arms, releasing a deluge of rain over Mrs. Loblolly, extinguishing the fire. Smoke filled the room.

"Abigail," I screamed over the downpour.

Pixel pounced from under the table, grabbing the hat in his teeth. He rolled around the floor, ripping at it with his claws.

"Tied by knots of thread, held by hands of dead, bound by earth, covered by dirt, lie eternal by woods." Abigail said as Pixel flew to the ceiling entangled with the shredded hat. Pixel and the hat fell to the floor with a thud.

Pixel stood up, shook himself off, and stared the hat down. "Bad hat," he scolded, giving it one more swipe with his paw before he turned his back and started cleaning himself.

Chattering away, the ladies settled back around the table as if nothing had happened.

Abigail stood still, her eyes on the hat. "What just happened?" she asked. "Am I crazy? Or did a possessed Halloween costume go crazy and tear up the cabin? Terra?"

"I-I…" I had no response.

"What are you all doing?" Abigail asked. "I don't know about you, but I'm shook and mad, really mad. Aren't you supposed to be the dream team? The League of Justice? The most powerful white magic in Asheville?"

"Abigail, calm down. This is why I've had you study the spell books. Magic cannot be destroyed, only transferred," I said, nuzzling up to her and rubbing against her. "The magic left by Mrs. Tangledwood's passing was absorbed by her hat. The dark creatures we woke in these mountains craved that magic. They would use it for evil. Mrs. Tangledwood left that magic for us. Magic is neither white nor black, evil nor good. It is how we use it and who commands it."

"I miss Emma. She was such a good friend," Doris Stickman said, her eyes clouding with tears. Although it had been over six months since Emma Tangledwood passed, the ladies still missed her. A gentle rain flowed over the table, focusing on Mrs. Stickman.

"Doris, you're doing it again," Mrs. Twiggs scolded.

"Oh dear, I'm sorry. I can't control my emotions." Mrs. Stickman held a handkerchief to her eyes.

Walking around the table, Mrs. Twiggs put her arm around Mrs. Stickman. "Bless your heart, Doris. I miss Emma too." She paused and then said, "Emma lives on in our hearts and through her legacy. She donated the proceeds from her estate to the preservation fund for the Biltmore Estate and its grounds. I'm stopping at the Tangledwood Estate tomorrow to help Miss Hartwell sort through her belongings for the upcoming estate sale."

I nudged her. "Yes, Terra, I know we have more urgent matters to discuss," Mrs. Twiggs said. "Terra, why don't you explain to our friends?"

I leaped onto the table. As I paced back and forth, I searched for the words that I could not find. "The black magic that took Mrs. Tangledwood opened a door for other magic to enter. The woods are awakening. I've seen shadows stirring. Shadows drawn to our white magic. They need to feed off us, drain us of our light." We all stared at the shredded hat. A dark cloud gathered over Mrs. Stickman. Pixel leaped into her lap, kneading her with paws and purring. "No fear. No fear. Terra fix."

Mrs. Stickman smiled. As quickly as it came, the dark cloud disappeared, and a small rainbow appeared in its stead. "I will be working with each of you individually to help you." I assured them with a confidence that I hoped I could live up to.

Abigail stood up and passed out spiral-bound notebooks to each of the ladies. The ladies browsed through the books, studying the handwritten recipes.

"These are basic spells, potions, incantations. All of them will help you focus on your individual powers," I explained, walking back and forth along the table.

Mrs. Loblolly raised her hand. "I can't read this. What language is it?"

"This is Ogham. It's an ancient language of the druids. Each of the stick symbols you see represents different trees. Each tree has different words associated with it, depending on how the symbols are arranged. The symbols themselves hold great power. They're still used on headstones to this date to open portals to different realms."

"If we can't read these spells, what good are they to us?" Mrs. Loblolly said.

"They're written in that language because very few can read

it, and I'm going to teach you all how to read Ogham starting tonight." I used my paw to point out a symbol in the book. "This symbol is for the rowan ash tree, my bloodline spirit tree." I pointed at the two adjacent symbols. "This is the oak, and this is the thorn. When the three combine, it makes the holy trinity of the fairy world."

Abigail stood up again, walking around the table. Standing behind Mrs. Stickman, she pulled back her silky black hair and placed a silver pendant around her neck. Mrs. Stickman examined the pendant, which was engraved with the oak, ash, and thorn trees. Abigail repeated this, placing a pendant on each woman. "These will help protect you as you learn. Their strength comes from our strength. Those pendants are all formed from the same piece of silver. The woman who owned this cabin owned that silver. She blessed it and enchanted it," I said, remembering Agatha Hollows hiding the silver in her storehouse so the soldiers would not find it.

"Tea anyone?" Mrs. Twiggs carried a tea service to the table and began pouring, releasing a sweet fragrance similar to apple blossoms.

"Is this part of the ceremony?" Mrs. Bartlett asked, accepting the cup from Mrs. Twiggs.

"No, just something to soothe our nerves. A little chamomile."

"To understand the power of the silver pendants, you must first understand the woman who enchanted it," I said. "Agatha Hollows trained as a Cherokee medicine woman, yet she wasn't Cherokee. Agatha befriended the Cherokee during the time of the Trail of Tears as the Cherokee were forced to leave their homes. She was summoned by their cries."

"Summoned?" Mrs. Raintree asked. "My people believed the winds were alive with spirits and could call to them."

I stared at her. She stopped herself from asking the unspoken question, instead saying, "Terra, I've been catching some very disturbing dreams in my dream catcher. Nightmares, really. Being chased through the woods, hunted. The faster I try to run, the slower I advance. The ground swallows me up."

"Wanda, I've had that dream too," Mrs. Bowers said. "Except I'm not running through the woods, I'm in town shopping. It's a beautiful day. I'm strolling along the shop fronts in Pack Square, but I feel someone watching me. I quicken my pace, and then suddenly the noisy street is quiet and I'm the only one around. The street opens up, engulfing me."

I saw by their expressions that all the ladies of the Biltmore Society were sharing the same or similar nightmare. Its meaning eluded me. Wiccans' dreams can be more real than reality. Their waking hours are veiled by the humans they walk among. As the ladies' bloodline has thinned through the centuries by mixing with mortal blood, the human world has become more real than the Wiccan world. They cannot see the magic that surrounds them. The wonder that this world and the next hold for them. In their dreams the true world awakens.

"Terra, what about the ninth Wiccan we need to complete our circle? You said a true coven has nine," Mrs. Stickman said.

"The ninth will find us when it's time," I told her. "While we wait, we will concentrate on strengthening your individual powers. Study your notebooks, learn your potions and incantations."

Mrs. Twiggs brought out a three-tier tray of homemade butter cookies. Pixel swiped his paw and knocked one off onto the floor and then moaned when Tracker gobbled it up. "Bad Tracker. Bad Tracker," Pixel scolded, swatting the puppy with a paw. Tracker's ghost violet eyes did not blink. Even though Pixel and Tracker had become great companions, lines were drawn when it came to table scraps, especially baked goods.

"I'll stop by each of your homes to help you with your training," I said.

Mrs. Twiggs continued stirring her cauldron in the fire. "I just can't get this right." She turned to the ladies.

I leaped off the table and ran to the cauldron. Standing on my back paws, I took a deep breath. "It's missing hogweed."

"Hogweed?" Mrs. Twiggs repeated. "There's no mention of hogweed in the recipe."

"These recipes have changed throughout the centuries. They need tweaking, or sometimes the person writing them down might have left off an ingredient. I can smell hogweed is missing, and it feels to me as if that is what is needed," I said.

"Where do I find hogweed?"

"The hogweed we need is not found in North Carolina. What we need was originally from Asia and then brought to Ontario as an ornamental plant. We're going to have to visit Karen Owen."

Mrs. Twiggs returned to the kitchen. Instead of more tea, she brought out sherry glasses and a decanter. As the women talked and cackled into the night, I sat by the fire with Abigail, who held Pixel on her lap. I thought about what Pixel had said and how the potion had awoken something in him even though I knew it had no strength.

"What wrong, Terra, what wrong? Why you look at me? Pixel bad?" Pixel leaped off Abigail's lap, tackling me and biting my ear. "Sorry about cookie."

I couldn't help but laugh. The whole world could be crumbling down around us, and Pixel would still be worried about a cookie crumb. His bravery and his appetite had no bounds.

Abigail smiled, watching us tumble and wrestle. Pixel made me feel more cat than witch. I gave into my feline urges when he was around.

Abigail and I waited on the front porch as Mrs. Twiggs said good night to the ladies and walked them out to their cars. Abigail sat on the rocking chair with Tracker at her feet. I sat on the railing, watching as the ladies drove into the night, my tail slashing like a metronome keeping time. In the distance I could hear the cracking of the oaks, thorn, and ash as the enchanted trees opened the road, allowing the ladies to pass. As quickly as they went by, the trees closed back over the road.

"Double, double toil and trouble." Abigail glanced up as she stirred her tea. "Fire burn and cauldron bubble."

I turned to stare at her. "Anne Hathaway was a witch. Her family name was Hawthorne. You don't think Shakespeare came up with that line himself, do you? His wife was more than his muse. Many of the great women in history were witches."

"I was kidding. I didn't mean anything."

"Be careful what words you speak, Abigail Oakhaven. For a witch as powerful as you, words hold great magic."

Abigail shrugged and retreated into the cabin, leaving me in the darkness.

THE GOLDEN SPOON

October 31, 1862,
Agatha Hollows's cabin,
Black Mountain, North Carolina

"TAKE WHAT YOU NEED, BUT leave me enough for the winter," Agatha gasped out, her words cutting through her pain. Blood stained her sleeve. I huddled in the corner, waiting to pounce.

The Confederate lieutenant examined her wound, his hand lingering. She winced as he squeezed her arm. "It's just a nick. I'll be fine," she said, pushing his hand away.

"We've come to commandeer supplies for the effort," he said, opening a large grain sack, then walking cautiously toward Agatha. I feared it wasn't food he sought. We heard a noise. The lieutenant turned to a young private, standing in the doorway.

The private spoke. "Sir, we have to leave her something."

The lieutenant raised his whip, and the private cringed, lowering his eyes before leaving. From across the yard, I heard the heavy door of the storehouse opening.

The lieutenant sat down across from Agatha. She drew back from him, cringing. There was something about him, more than the deformity that he wore with pleasure. He seemed to enjoy the terror. He smiled. "Mrs. Hollows, ma'am, it's not safe for you to be out here on your own." His soft Southern drawl held a grit to it. Agatha shifted in her rocking chair next to the blazing fire.

"I'm going to bring you back to Asheville." The lieutenant bent down next to her chair. I could smell the foul stench of gangrene. Agatha stirred the fire. "Can I get you some tea?" Not waiting for an answer, she poured cups of nettle tea. Then she reached in the dry sink, pulling out a small gold teaspoon given to her by a wealthy Ashevillian she had healed. The only item she had of value. With a slow hand, she placed the teacups on the table. "Sugar," she asked. The lieutenant didn't answer. She scooped sugar into his teacup, stirring it with the gold spoon.

He stared at Agatha as she stirred his teacup with the gold spoon. Then he pushed himself away from the table and stood. "We'll be back," he said, stepping toward the door.

As the door closed behind him, Agatha collapsed in her chair. I jumped onto her lap. "The spoon as I feared. Terra, he's a hunter," Agatha said. "Never let him know your true identity. It's too late for me."

"Agatha, what about the gold spoon? What are you talking about?" I asked.

I watched as Agatha gathered her remaining belongings. She ran to the herb shed carefully choosing what to bring with her. "What do you mean hunter? Where are you going?" I asked.

Not stopping to answer, Agatha collected several jars and ran into the cabin. I sat on the rocking chair by the fire and watched in silence. Agatha stopped for a moment and put her hands on her hips. She gazed around the tiny cabin. It had been her home since she had escaped from the Trail of Tears, the forced eviction of the Cherokee from their mountain to the west.

Over the years we had been together, she had become a mentor and a friend, as much of a friend as she would allow. She taught me with her actions more than her words. I watched carefully as she healed the mountain folk and spoke with the spirits in the woods.

I had not asked her for her help in my turning back to my true form. There was only one witch who could change me back to a girl—no, *a* witch. Elizabeth, leader of my coven. It had been nearly two centuries since Elizabeth and my sisters met their fate. I felt in my blood that they did not die a true death. They drifted into the other realm. I glanced up to see Agatha staring at me.

"Elizabeth will find you, Terra. She's searching for you. There's a darkness, a shadow that hides you from her. Find her bloodline and you will find her."

"Where will you go?"

Agatha ran into the bedroom. I watched as she removed the floorboard under the bed and retrieved an old parchment. She placed it on the table, grabbed the lantern, and held it close. On it was a drawing of a field of flowers and in the very distance a bridge. She sat down, examining the drawing, running her finger along it. Then she stood, holding her gnarled hands by the fire, still stained with her blood. The vessel that held her was old and withered, merely a façade to put the humans at ease. Humans rarely took notice of the elderly. "Across the border into South Carolina to Glassy Mountain. The Confederate deserters and northern sympathizers take refuge in the Dark Corner." Agatha paused, smiled, and went to the door. She stopped and retrieved the gold spoon and then grabbed her sack and left the cabin. Her dogs waited on the porch. "Go, my children, keep your bloodline in these woods," she said as she kissed each dog's head. They sat still and watched us leave.

A BLOOD RELATIVE

Tangledwood Estate, Biltmore Forest

I ACCOMPANIED MRS. TWIGGS TO MRS. Tangledwood's. I knew it would be a difficult day for her. Mrs. Tangledwood had been her dear, dear friend. We rode up the long driveway in Mrs. Twiggs's Volvo. Inspired by the nearby Biltmore Estate, Mrs. Tangledwood's brick-and-stucco French chateau style rose up to greet us. Adorning its rooftop were six peaked gables. Over the massive door hung a gargoyle. Mrs. Twiggs politely knocked with the heavy brass doorknocker. The ten-foot-high hand-carved wooden door opened slowly with a creak. The young housekeeper, donned in ripped jeans and T-shirt, curtsied. This attire would not have been acceptable if Mrs. Tangledwood were still here. "Mrs. Twiggs, Miss Hartwell is expecting you," she said, pointing in the direction of the library.

Mrs. Twiggs's practical heels clicked on the Italian marble of the great foyer as we went to the library, which was adjacent to the winding staircase. The room was circular, lined with mahogany bookshelves. Mrs. Tangledwood had shared Mrs. Twiggs's love of books and delighted in collecting old, rare editions, especially those on mysticism, magic, and mayhem.

Unlike the housekeeper, Miss Hartwell maintained her professional appearance, dressed in a smart pantsuit of navy-blue silk with a white blouse. Her brown hair was kept short and neat. She was not unattractive for a woman of nearly sixty. She was—had been—Mrs. Tangledwood's personal assistant, confidante, and in the waning years, her nurse. Mrs. Tangledwood's will had named her executor, so she stayed on to help with the estate sale. She sat in a red leather chair by the fireplace, which did not please Mr. Tangledwood. I had seen him several times before sitting in that very chair—it was his favorite. He gave her a disgusted look and then disappeared into the wall.

"Miss Hartwell." Mrs. Twiggs stepped across the Persian rug to greet the woman.

"Mrs. Twiggs, so good of you to come."

Mrs. Twiggs went to sit in the leather chair next to Miss Hartwell in the chair Mr. Tangledwood was about to sit in. He jumped up with another disgruntled look on his face and disappeared back into the wall, leaving the faint smell of cloves. Mrs. Twiggs sniffed. She had not seen him, but I'm sure she felt him.

"I think we have everything organized for the sale. I've had the staff inventorying and tagging items," Miss Hartwell said.

"Thank you, Miss Hartwell, it will make it a lot easier for us the day of the sale. Preparation is always appreciated." Mrs. Twiggs smiled.

"There are some items, however, that Mrs. Tangledwood left for her friends and family."

"Family?"

"Yes, of course. Her great-niece Charlotte arrived yesterday."

"Oh?" Mrs. Twiggs appeared confused. "Emma never talked much about her family, a sore subject she would say."

"Let me go get Charlotte." Miss Hartwell left the room.

Mrs. Twiggs turned to me. "Terra, Emma's bloodline."

Before I could answer, Miss Hartwell came back with a young twenty-something girl who shared Mrs. Tangledwood's auburn hair. I had only known Mrs. Tangledwood the elder, but I could see the resemblance and imagined a young Mrs. Tangledwood. Charlotte's features were pleasant; her stature was slight, no more than five feet I'd say. She seemed fit and healthy. She wore a proper yellow cashmere sweater set and pencil skirt, almost too proper for a girl of her age, but then I was used to seeing Abigail wearing tattered jeans, biker boots, and leather coats. The girls of this era lay no claim to style. "Mrs. Twiggs, this is Charlotte Tangledwood."

Charlotte smiled and extended her hand. Mrs. Twiggs grasped it, giving her a warm smile. "Oh, my dear, you are a young Emma, aren't you? I can't begin to tell you how pleased I am to meet you."

"U-uh," Charlotte stuttered, shifting from foot to foot. "I... only met my great-aunt once when I was very young. I didn't know her. I didn't even know of her death until Miss Hartwell contacted me."

Still holding her hand, Mrs. Twiggs said, "Please come sit down. Tell me everything about yourself."

Charlotte glanced back at Miss Hartwell, who guided them back to the chairs by the fireplace. "There's not much to tell, Mrs. Twiggs," Charlotte said.

"Please, dear, call me Beatrice. Start with your family."

"My parents died when I was little. I was raised by a foster family. I was told that DCFS reached out to my aunt but never heard back."

"Oh, my dear, that's terrible. It doesn't sound like Emma. She was very compassionate."

"From what I understand, there was a lot of family fighting and they weren't very close—my parents and her. I came to pay my respects and put closure on it, you know."

"You're Emma's family, which means you're our family now and you're most welcome."

I smelled the clove and turned to see Mr. Tangledwood in the far corner behind the rosewood writing desk, puffing away on his imaginary pipe. He had only passed some twenty years ago, and as many young ghosts, he didn't realize he had crossed over and was continuing his human habits despite a lengthy battle with lung cancer. He saw me staring at him, snuffed out his imaginary pipe, and disappeared out the window.

"Miss Hartwell had a room made up for me. I'm going to stay for the estate sale and the closing of the will," Charlotte said.

"The Ladies of the Biltmore Society, a garden club you might say that your great-aunt chaired, will be anxious to meet you. We'll have to throw a party," Mrs. Twiggs said.

Charlotte smiled.

A GRAND REOPENING

Biltmore Village

NESTLED IN THE MOUNTAINS WHERE the Swannanoa River flows into the French Broad was Biltmore Village, formerly known as the town of Best and before that it was home to the Cherokee. That all changed when George Vanderbilt began construction on his great estate and needed homes for the craftsmen required to build it. Biltmore Village was modeled after a small English village, providing a fitting and quaint entrance to the Biltmore Estate.

In the middle of the village, the green was being mowed for the upcoming May Day celebration. In the early 1900s, the parish school erected a maypole and a flower-adorned throne for the May queen, a celebration the ladies were bringing back this spring.

Stepping along the uneven cobblestone sidewalk, we reached the Leaf & Page, standing as it had for over a century. It was hard to distinguish from the others as all the homes, now storefronts, were built from brick, stucco, pebbledash, and wood timber, giving the building an old-world charm in this new-world town. In the etched glass of the picture window, Mrs. Twiggs displayed first editions related to the Vanderbilt family, the Biltmore Estate and Asheville along with her jars of exotic teas. Mrs. Twiggs unlocked the door of the Leaf & Page. I hurried in behind her, Pixel behind me. Abigail pulled a cigarette out of her leather coat. As she raised it to her lips, I gave her a quick tap with my claw on her leg. She glared at me, harrumphing, and shoved the cigarette back in her pocket.

Mrs. Twiggs opened the door, flipping on the lights. We followed her inside. She strolled about the front room, opening the shutters, letting in the early morning sunlight. She walked behind the cash register counter and stared at the portrait of her late husband Albert. The picture blurred and swirled into a mist as Albert appeared in front of us. "My darling, you seem troubled," Albert said, levitating inches off the floor.

Mrs. Twiggs reached to embrace him. "Shadows and mist," I whispered.

Albert's memory was etched into the walls of the Leaf & Page. Mrs. Twiggs had always felt his presence, but since her turning, she could now see and communicate with him. She pulled back not able to touch him. "Albert, I miss you so."

"Beatrice, my love, we have many lives together before and after this world."

Mrs. Twiggs smiled. In his previous life, Albert had been a cynic, a lover of science, a pragmatist, but since his death he had become a believer.

A torn and tattered book floated off the shelf, landing on the counter, its pages flipped open. Mrs. Twiggs smiled and read the passage from *The Journal of Elizabeth Lightfoot Roadman Rankin*. "My beloved William struggles with the conflict. His friends and peers sympathize with the secession of the South, but he feels it will tear our beloved Asheville apart as others fight to keep the Union together. In hopes to quiet the hearts of our community, I am hosting a dinner to bring both sides together. Maybe they can come to peace."

Mrs. Twiggs closed the journal. "Terra, I've been asked by the curator at the Biltmore to help with their upcoming Civil War exhibit." Encompassing eight thousand acres, the Biltmore Estate was a grand mansion. Its two hundred fifty rooms made it the largest mansion in the United States, and it brought droves of tourists to Asheville. Their exhibits changed seasonally.

"Are you sure you're up to all this? Opening the store? Helping at the Biltmore?" I asked her.

Mrs. Twiggs fell onto a chair with a heavy thud. "It's not the same without Emma. She was the Biltmore Society. I feel I owe it to her to continue on." She patted the book in her lap. "This journal was written by the wife of a predominant Asheville businessman. She chronicled the events of Asheville before and during the Civil War. I hope it will help with the exhibit. They're bringing in an expert, a scholar from the University of Richmond, to curate."

Albert glided across the floor and sat down next to Mrs. Twiggs. He reached for the book but was unable to turn the pages. She held it out to him, hovering it above his lap. He skimmed the pages, his head nestled alongside hers.

I strolled across the top of the couch, listening as they read from the memoirs. They read late into the night, Mrs. Twiggs's head bouncing up and down, struggling to stay awake. Until finally sleep took her. I said good night to Albert as he vanished back into his portrait.

I heard moaning from the back room. I ran to find Pixel hunched up in a corner under a table. "Pixel, what's wrong?"

"Terra, Pixel scared."

"Scared of what?"

"That man. He not real."

"You can see Albert, Pixel?"

Pixel nodded his head.

"It's okay, Pixel, he's a friend."

"He not real, Terra."

"He's a ghost, Pixel, a good ghost. That's Mrs. Twiggs's husband."

"He dead?"

"He left this life, and he is living another, Pixel. He lived many lives."

"Pixel no understand."

I could hear his stomach growling. "How about we have a snack and I'll explain."

Pixel thought for a moment, scratched his chin, and said, "Pixel eat." He came out from under the table and circled around me. He made fast work of the butter cookies that Mrs. Twiggs had next to her tea. I watched him carefully. Something was not right. First the premonition, now he was able to see ghosts. These were abilities of the fairy world. Not seen nor understood by the humans who shared the earth. Animals especially cats can sense the spirit world; upon occasion they will sit perfectly still, staring at a wall. Cats' whiskers are like a tuning fork. They send out vibrations that attract spirits; in turn, the whiskers can sense the vibrations that spirits create as they part the molecules that comprise the waking world. Spirits, more so ghosts, as the humans call them, are memories and energy with no form in the physical realm. They appear as we expect them, as Mr. Twiggs, for example. He appears to his wife as he did in life, and I see him through his image from his portrait above the register. Pixel knew him not by either, yet he saw him in the form of a man as fairy folk would. That gave me great concern.

"What fairies, Terra?" he said, looking up with crumbs on his whiskers.

"I didn't think I thought that out loud." Curious and curiouser, I thought, stealing a line from Lewis Carroll.

Pixel finished his cookie. It was nearly midnight. Mrs. Twiggs would be up at five, preparing the store, making blueberry muffins. I could tell that the events of Halloween were a strain on her. She needed to return to normalcy, get back to her human routine. I curled up next to Pixel by the fire, its heat warming us, and drifted off.

When I woke, I heard Mrs. Twiggs bustling around the kitchen, Pixel underfoot.

"Me hungry. Me hungry," Pixel chanted repeatedly.

"It's coming, Pixel," Mrs. Twiggs said.

I sauntered into the kitchen, my tail swiping the wall as I entered. Pixel scurried in between Mrs. Twiggs's legs, his tail pointed upright, shaking ferociously. It was early, not quite dawn. But the announcement of the reopening of the Leaf & Page would bring all the regulars out hungry for Mrs. Twiggs's tea, scones, and muffins.

We followed Mrs. Twiggs out to her small garden behind the store. She opened the henhouse door. "Good morning, ladies," she said. I heard Pixel's stomach growl. I gave him a look. He smiled and lay down in the dewy grass. Mrs. Twiggs filled a basket with eggs and then stopped to check her herb garden. Fairy lights lit our way along the stepping-stone path. She stopped at a tiny fairy cottage and opened the door. She was not surprised to find no one at home. Mrs. Twiggs was a believer even before her magic was awakened. She knew that fairy tales were just that, a tale for children. Mrs. Twiggs, she was a child at heart.

Abigail was waiting for us in the kitchen. Mrs. Twiggs tied a white apron around Abigail's waist. "Let's give this a try, shall we?" They stood at the large butcher-block island where Mrs. Twiggs had measured out all the ingredients.

"Abigail, it's no different than mixing a potion," Mrs. Twiggs said, watching over Abigail's shoulder. "Baking is chemistry and following directions. First you mix the dry ingredients together, and then you combine the eggs, sugar, and butter."

Abigail carefully scooped flour into a measuring cup, half of it landing on the counter.

"That's a good start, dear. You'll get it."

Pixel watched intensely from the small kitchen table.

Abigail wiped her brow, leaving a white tread mark across her forehead.

"Seriously, you've never baked before," I asked, leaving white paw prints on the counter.

"Yes, Terra, I'm sure back in your day everything was real farm to table. What's the point when I can stop at a bakery?" Abigail said.

"You know, Abigail, the way to a man's heart…"

Abigail interrupted me and said, "Terra, when was the last time you baked for a man?" She then paused and said, "Oh geez, I'm sorry. I wasn't thinking. I'm frustrated. It's getting late and I'm way behind. Honestly I don't know what I'm doing."

I took a deep breath. I never had the chance to bake for a man or dance or get married. I never felt a kiss upon my lips, and I didn't know if I ever would. I felt the need to be alone. I hopped off the counter and ran into the alley. I ran past the dumpster and then stopped, going back to gaze into the broken mirror someone had discarded. No matter how many times I saw my image I was always surprised. In my mind I was still a seventeen-year-old girl, not this ordinary gray alley cat. I had been taking out my frustrations on Abigail, pushing her to succeed where I couldn't, pushing her to live the life I couldn't. I was afraid to admit it, but somewhere deep inside I hoped that if I could help Abigail become the witch her great-grandmother was, she could find a way to turn me back. I was so deep in thought I didn't realize Pixel sat next to me, staring at his reflection in the mirror. He put his paw around me. "Terra, you pretty."

I let out a low growl and then realized he was trying to cheer me up. "Thank you, Pixel," I said.

We hurried back to the Leaf & Page. The sun would be rising shortly, and I'm sure there would be a crowd of hungry customers. We slipped in through the cat door. Abigail was taking the muffins out of the oven. She knelt down and picked me up. "I'm so sorry, Terra. It must be so frustrating for you. To be around me. I promise I'll try harder."

I wiped the flour off her nose with my paw and nuzzled my head against her shoulder. Mrs. Twiggs came over and hugged us both.

She then opened the front door to let the stream of customers in. Mrs. Twiggs greeted each one as though they were old friends; some were while others were new. They all remarked how wonderful she looked. The enchantment of their turning gave the ladies a youthful glow. Mrs. Twiggs couldn't disguise the spring in her step. To them she looked eighty years old, but she moved like a prima ballerina. Pixel sat on the edge of the counter, a furry gargoyle watching the commotion. Now and then an elderly woman would walk up and rub his belly. At first he was offended, but then he would roll onto his back and purr.

When everyone had been fed, Mrs. Twiggs tapped her teacup with her spoon. "May I please have your attention?"

The crowded room fell silent, and all eyes turned to her.

"I wanted to thank you all for joining me for the reopening of the Leaf & Page. Please help yourself to muffins and tea on me today." She winked at Albert.

As the cuckoo struck five, Mrs. Twiggs escorted the last patron out and flipped the sign to CLOSED. She bustled into the kitchen and filled the three-tier cookie tray with an assortment of fresh-baked cookies, bringing them to the large sideboard in the dining room. She placed chairs around the table, stopping to gaze at the room. It had a festive air. Abigail had hung streamers from the crystal chandelier and placed balloons on the table. Mrs. Twiggs next brought out a crystal punch bowl filled with sparkling champagne punch. Curled up on the table, Pixel reached out his paw nonchalantly, inching his way to the punch bowl.

"Pixel," Mrs. Twiggs screamed at him from across the room. He turned with an orange sherbet mustache, his orange saucer eyes wide open. He fell off the table with a thud. He mumbled under his breath, shook himself off, and went back to his place by the fire.

As the clock struck six, the cars pulled up in front, jockeying for position on the crowded street. Mrs. Twiggs greeted each of the ladies with a hug, taking their coats and hanging them by the front door. She led them into the dining room, passing out cups of champagne punch. When they all had been served, Mrs. Twiggs said, "Ladies, please settle down." The conversation ebbed into a single ongoing argument between Mrs. Loblolly and Mrs. Branchworthy, regarding family sides blue and gray. From listening to them, it sounded as if the Civil War were still being fought.

Mrs. Twiggs tapped her glass again while giving them an old schoolmarm stern glance. The ladies quieted down. Mrs. Twiggs cleared her throat and said, "Now, ladies, I know we all have questions for Charlotte, Emma's niece. She came as quite a surprise to me, but I think it's important we make her feel welcome, so let's not overwhelm her."

The ladies nodded in agreement, saying, "Yes," "Certainly," and "Of course." The silver bell over the transom tinkled. Abigail glanced up, ran to greet Miss Hartwell and Charlotte. Abigail stopped and gave Charlotte the once-over. She was dressed in a designer wrap dress. Abigail smoothed out her rumpled T-shirt and glanced at the holes in her jeans. "Hi, I'm Abigail, Abigail Oakhaven."

"Charlotte Tangledwood." They nodded at each other.

"Okay," Abigail said, taking Miss Hartwell's light jacket and hanging it up. Miss Hartwell followed the noise into the dining room.

"I've always wanted to be invited to a meeting of the Ladies of the Biltmore Society," Miss Hartwell said, entering the room where Mrs. Twiggs greeted her with a punch glass.

Abigail stayed behind to talk to Charlotte. "Hey, I wanted to warn you, they've all been talking about you and have a lot of questions."

"You don't have a smoke on you, do you?" Charlotte asked.

Abigail glanced behind to make sure I wasn't watching, grabbed her leather jacket off the rack, and said, "Let's go out front."

I slipped out with them. I had to monitor Abigail to make sure she didn't say anything until we knew who or what Charlotte was.

They sat on the wood bench in front of the store. It was an unseasonably cool evening for late April. I gazed at Abigail with narrow, disapproving eyes. She lit her cigarette and Charlotte's anyway. "Is that your cat?" Charlotte asked.

"Not my cat. Kind of a mascot. She hangs around the store." Abigail shrugged.

I emitted a low hiss and swiped at her.

"Not very friendly, is she?" Charlotte asked in between puffs.

They finished their cigarettes, putting them out on the ground before going back inside. "We better get this over with," Abigail said.

The two girls stepped into the dining room. I tagged along behind them. "There you are," Mrs. Twiggs said. "Charlotte, these are the Ladies of the Biltmore Society, dear friends of your great-aunt's."

Charlotte shyly waved.

I heard a rustling in the storage room. The door was cracked. I peeked in to see a shadow crawling up the wall. I watched as the tail disappeared into the shadow mouth and Pixel muttered, "Yummy." I felt my stomach growl. No matter how much I fight the feline urges, they still take me. I wanted to join in the hunt with Pixel.

I heard footsteps outside the storage room. I smelled Miss Hartwell and Charlotte. "Let's make an early evening of it. There's a lot to do before the estate sale," Miss Hartwell said. "These old hens will be cackling all night."

"Okay, Miss Hartwell," Charlotte said.

After all the ladies had left, Mrs. Twiggs locked the door and settled onto the chair by the fire, raising her feet onto the stool. Abigail sat across from her, an early copy of *Tom Sawyer* in her lap. I jumped on the back of the chair and peered over her shoulder, purring. I had met its author on my earlier travels and found him charming.

Abigail reached up and rubbed my chin. My eyes closed, and sleep took me.

1862

Asheville Highway

I KNOW I'M DREAMING. THE REASON I know I'm dreaming is because I'm walking behind Agatha Hollows. I remember
this trail from Asheville into South Carolina. She said nothing as
we walked, our feet laden with the weight of the heavy red clay
that clings to us. An occasional wagon passes our way, pushing us
to the side and deeper into the mud. Agatha doesn't rest. I am cold,
and my fur is coated with the mud. My steps are heavy with its
weight, but I won't stop. I won't let Agatha know I'm in pain, but
I sense from her stooped shoulders that she feels the same pain. We
hear horses behind us, closing in at a quick pace. Agatha hides in
the tall pines lining the road. We watch as the gray coats ride by.
It is twilight. She searches the sky trying to fix her direction, then
continues deep into the woods. She walks light-footed, no snapping twigs, no footprints behind her, as though not touching the
ground. My eyes close as I walk, relying on my sense of smell and
hearing. It's now pitch-black; a blue-black darkness covers the stars
and there is no moon to give light. Agatha settles under a white
oak. I want to wake up. I don't like this part. I know what happens

next, and I don't want to remember. I feel a bite on my neck and open my eyes to see Pixel.

"Bad dream, Terra, bad dream," he scolds.

Pixel's moist saucers stared into my eyes. "Go away." I swatted at him with one paw. "Pixel, I'm okay, go away." Cats don't cry, but if we did I think Pixel would have shed a tear. He looked so crestfallen. He has such a good heart I feel bad when I scold him, but the dream left me in a bad mood. It was almost as draining as the dreams from when I was a girl back in Salem.

The fire had died out and the room was cold. The cuckoo clock behind the register sang three times for three a.m., the witching hour. I smiled to myself. Nothing to worry about. After all I am a witch. Elizabeth had once told me the history behind the witching hour. Goodness taken from the earth two thousand years ago at three p.m. Evil walks the opposite of that time. A myth I thought when I was a little girl, but since my turning I've seen many dark creatures during the witching hour. The humans don't know the difference between white magic and black magic. That's why the Ladies of the Biltmore Society must keep their secret. My coven in Salem did not keep the secret, and it cost them their mortal lives and led me to my current form. "Pixel," I yelled out. "I'm sorry."

Pixel sat in the doorway between the reading room and dining room, his back turned to me. The twitching of his tail was the only indication he had heard me. I did have a bad dream, and it left me in a grumpy mood.

"Grumpy cat," Pixel said, running over to tackle me. We had watched a video on YouTube of a grumpy cat. Pixel found him hysterical.

Mrs. Twiggs would be waking in a few hours and would start her preparations for the day. She needed to keep busy.

"Pixel. I think the store is in good hands. We need to return to the cabin," I said.

"Abigail," Pixel said.

"Yes, Abigail needs us." She had left the party early. I had a sudden premonition. It was calling me back to the cabin and to Abigail, who was alone with only Tracker the dog to guard her. We hurried out through the cat door into the alley. The others were asleep. Children of the street, cats and dogs. Pixel's white chest glowed in the dark. His orange-and-white-striped tail wiggled back and forth as we trotted through the alleyways. We hurried past the park and into the Montford District with its eclectic mixture of Victorian, craftsman, and bungalows all built in the early days when Asheville was a seasonal resort. I stopped. "Moonlight."

"What, Terra?"

"Montford. It smells like moonlight."

"How smell?"

I thought about Lionel, a dear friend, a watcher, a victim of the darkness that had entered Asheville. This was our favorite neighborhood, and he was the one who had told me it smelled like moonlight. I didn't quite understand until I smelled the same scent on Abigail. The smell of history, the smell of elegance, the smell of mystery. The sun rose over the mountain laurels, their twisted branches climbing to reach it and up Black Mountain. As we reached the cabin, Pixel yelled with glee. He could smell the bacon. He ran up the stairs before me and pushed open the door. Abigail stood over the potbellied stove with an iron skillet full of sizzling back bacon. Tracker was glued to her side, waiting for a slip of the hand.

Abigail sat down, sipping her coffee. "I woke up last night at three. Bryson was hovering over my bed, inches from my face. He was saying something, but I couldn't understand. His mouth moved, but no words came out. The only word I heard was Charlotte. Then he was gone."

I leaped onto the table and rubbed my neck against Abigail's arm to calm her. I knew she needed me. "Bryson is your watcher. He watches out for you. Charlotte plays some role in our lives that I cannot see yet."

"Terra, I wasn't afraid. I liked Bryson when he was in this world. I'm beginning to understand that there are more worlds than just this one." Abigail was becoming a witch, more powerful than her great-grandmother, my Elizabeth. There would be no limits to her abilities, but with that came responsibility and she still was just a girl. Pixel was onto his third piece of bacon before we realized what he was doing. Abigail lifted him off the table and put him on the floor next to Tracker, who let out a low growl. Pixel swatted Tracker's nose before taking off.

"Terra, I wanted to show you something I found." Abigail hurried into the bedroom and returned with a book. One I did not recall seeing before.

"Where did you find that?"

"I found it under the floorboards under my bed."

"It was Agatha Hollows's book," I said.

She placed the book on the table. A green mist seeped out of its spine as it flipped open. What I recognized were spells spewed from its pages, the language undecipherable. The numbers and letters danced around our heads, trying to line up on a chalkboard.

"I can't understand any of these spells. They're in some language I've never seen before." Abigail shook her head. She slammed the book closed.

"The book is enchanted, Abigail. You won't be able to read it." I had tried for years to read Agatha's spell books, hoping to find the one spell that would bring me back to my true form. All my attempts had failed. Agatha was not from this world. "Only Agatha could read it."

"Where is she now?"

"I lost her." It was difficult to speak the words. Remembering the events in my dreams was difficult enough, but it was more difficult to speak about them in daylight.

"Lost her?"

"She left her human form."

Abigail gave me a quizzical glance. Pixel jumped back onto the table, and Abigail stroked his back.

"Agatha was drawn to the Cherokee people. She was part of the woods. Cherokee believe that spirits live in the woods and can change forms. She changed her form to escape the soldiers."

"Why?"

"They wanted to command her powers, and she couldn't let that happen."

Pixel spilled sugar on the table, giggled, and scooped it up with his paw. "Mmm, sweet," Pixel said.

"Terra, I want to show you something." Abigail hurried out of the cabin, Tracker on her heels, heading down into the valley. Pixel and I caught up to her. The valley was waking from its winter sleep, the trees starting to bud, the only thing in bloom the bright purple blue of the heather. "Tracker and I were walking this morning and found this. Isn't it strange? Everything else is dormant."

"I've never seen this on the mountain before. That's a good sign.

The Irish witches used heather to ward off evil," I said.

Pixel jumped into the heather, rolling and tumbling. Tracker followed, emitting low growls. Abigail and I returned to the cabin. She lit a fire under the cauldron. She repeated the recipe that Mrs. Twiggs had been mixing. I sniffed. "Where did you find hogweed?"

"I found it next to the spell book under my bed under the floorboards." Before I could stop her, Abigail scooped up a ladle and took a sip. Instantly her eyes rolled back in her head. She levitated off the floor. Her aura turned bright white so white I had to avert my eyes. The cabin shook, and then she fell to the ground. I raced to her side. "Abigail," I shouted.

"Terra, what happened? I never felt anything like that before." Abigail sat up, shaking out her arms.

"You're not gifted with premonition. You shouldn't drink that potion. Bottle it, and we'll bring it to Mrs. Twiggs."

MRS. LUND

Biltmore Estate

RELUCTANTLY I ALLOWED MRS. TWIGGS to put on my emotional support animal vest. Pixel liked his. He thought himself handsome and important. We needed them to join the ladies for tea at the Biltmore Estate. We sat in the meeting room at the Biltmore surrounded by the ladies who were on time for high tea and cakes. Mrs. Twiggs read the order of the ceremony, which dated back to Frederick Law Olmsted. "He brought his vision of the world to Asheville; the secret gardens hold the mysteries of the corners of the world. We celebrate and honor him today." The ladies raised their teacups and nodded.

The meeting began. "Today's agenda is the Civil War exhibit. I know many of you ladies have artifacts from family members who served on either side. The Biltmore would appreciate your loaning them for the exhibit." She swallowed before continuing, "To help curate the exhibit is our special guest, Professor Lund from Richmond University. She's an expert on North Carolina's history during the Civil War."

Seated next to Mrs. Twiggs was a woman of some age, her gray hair pulled back in a bun, her thick black glasses required after years of reading textbooks. She was dressed in a modest gray suit. She looked like a history professor should. She stood and greeted the ladies. "Thank you, all, for the warm welcome. I'm eager to hear more about each of your family histories especially yours, Mrs. Loblolly." She smiled at Mrs. Loblolly, who nodded graciously. "I've read extensive reports on your four-times-removed grandfather, Colonel Odysseus Loblolly of the Seventh Carolina."

Mrs. Loblolly raised her teacup. She was very proud of her heritage. She motioned to the large bag on the floor next to her. "I've brought some swords, uniforms, and journals to share with you."

As Professor Lund spoke, my eyes grew heavy. The warm tea and even hotter room made it difficult to stay awake. My ears perked up when I heard Professor Lund speak of the Asheville Trail. She continued, "Many Northern sympathizers and Confederate deserters crossed the border to South Carolina across the trail. Asheville was a transportation hub in the early 1860s for the war."

My eyes drifted closed again. I dreamed. I could hear the wagon wheels churning up the red mud as they crossed the border. Its occupants ever on the lookout for the gray coats. Agatha greeted the travelers and chose to ride with them, hoping there was safety in numbers. I leaped into the back of the wagon by the children—five of early ages. Agatha sat on the driver's bench with the man and woman. I smelled the herbs that Agatha had brought with her. It was a comforting smell, and then I smelled something else, alcohol. I rummaged through the sacks to find brass tubing and a mason jar. Agatha Hollows had a still of her own by the cabin for medicinal purposes, so I knew what this was. I heard the driver say they were headed to Packs Mountain. We stopped for the night and made camp. The travelers shared their beans and fatback with Agatha, who in turned shared with me. She sat next to the fire, poking it with a stick. The young girl rocking in her mother's arms coughed repeatedly. Agatha stood up and went over to the girl. The mother gazed up protectively but then handed the child to Agatha, who sat back down by the fire cross-legged with the child on her lap. She listened to her chest. "This girl has consumption." She reached into her pack and pulled out a jar with some herbs, crumbling them in her hands. Then she spit into the leaves and made a paste. She rubbed it on the child's chest, whispered in her ear, and then the coughing stopped. Her mother rushed over, beaming. "She's been coughing for almost a week."

Agatha put the paste into a jar, handed it to the mother. "Put this on her every night. She'll be fine in a few days."

The children's father watched, smoking a pipe from his seat across the other side of the fire. We drifted off in front of the fire, the long day's travel exhausting us.

By next day's end, we reached a ridge. "Packs Mountain Ridge," I heard the man say.

We headed up. The evening air cooled the ground, sending up a mist. The path was a razorback of granite and red earth. No more than a couple hundred feet across, dropping off sharply on both sides. A very defendable fortress. As we climbed, I saw the far Appalachian Mountains of Tennessee to the south and Glassy Mountain to the north. We settled at the top. The man unloaded the still and began constructing his livelihood. The woman settled the children and started a fire. Agatha and I watched as she made supper. "Agatha, we should leave," I said.

"Terra, they know not what they do," she replied.

The woman saw Agatha rubbing her arthritic hands and brought her a jar of moonshine. Agatha smiled and then sniffed it. Then she poured it out on the ground. "You took this too early. The first five percent is poison. The next thirty percent you pull is the head, smells strong, burns your nose, but drinkable if needed. Wait for the heart, that's the next thirty percent, that'll smell sweet, brings you the best price."

The man ran over and slapped Agatha hard across the face. She swayed back from the impact. "Old woman, that was good shine you spilled." He then turned to his wife and with a closed fist punched her in the eye. She fell to her knees.

After the man left, Agatha placed a compress of herbs on the woman's eye. She then handed her a small vial. "If it gets to be more than you can stand, put this in his drink."

The woman looked back at the man, then smiled at Agatha and took the vial. When we woke, the man was gone. Agatha gathered her things. "Wait, where are you going? You can ride with us," the mother said, balancing the sick girl on her hip.

Agatha shook her head, knowing better. We thanked her and left.

We made it deep into South Carolina when the gray coat hunters led by the man reached us. Thirty pieces of silver, I thought, the going price for betrayal.

My eyes half-open, I could see Mrs. Twiggs talking to Mrs. Lund. When I woke, Mrs. Branchworthy was raising her voice. "It was a hundred and fifty years ago."

Mrs. Branchworthy's family had fought on opposite sides of the war than Mrs. Loblolly's, and the two had been in conflict for years. As Mrs. Branchworthy spoke, I saw a puff of gray smoke circling around her. Mrs. Twiggs rushed to calm her. I didn't think Mrs. Lund had noticed. She seemed embarrassed over the ladies' argument. Pulling herself together, Mrs. Branchworthy sat back down, her hands leaving a scorch mark on the walnut table. "I'm so sorry, Mrs. Lund," she said.

Mrs. Lund smiled.

Mrs. Twiggs stood up, gathered her purse, and said her goodbyes. I followed her out of the front entrance, past the tourists gazing at the large structure. We entered the garden, the tulips in full bloom. Pixel chased butterflies. Mrs. Twiggs and I sat down on a bench overlooking the bass pond. "Terra, aren't the tulips beautiful?"

Tulips, I thought. I remembered Agatha warming them up and placing them on insect bites to take away the sting.

"Terra, how do we keep the secret? The ladies couldn't keep a secret before they became Wiccans. How do you expect them to keep it now? And how do we keep people from finding out?"

"People see what they want to see. Humans don't believe in magic. That's why they can't see that it is all around them."

Mrs. Twiggs hesitated. "But what if Mrs. Branchworthy had started a fire? What if she burned the Biltmore to the ground?"

"We'll work on her control and her temper," I assured her.

A PREMONITION

PIXEL AND I LAY IN the bed next to Mrs. Twiggs. The tiny bedroom above the Leaf & Page was cozy and warm. As of late, Pixel and I had taken to sharing the double bed with Mrs. Twiggs. I believe she felt it as comforting as we did. In the corner the rocking chair rocked slowly. Albert sat watching her sleep as he had for the past ten years since his passing. I could see the sadness and feel his love. Even though now after her turning Mrs. Twiggs could see Albert, she couldn't feel his caress or tender kiss. Albert was not a watcher like the others. He was not assigned to his Wiccan. His was a deeper calling—true love. As it is when all beings cross over to the next plain, he achieved enlightenment. He knew before her what she was and what she was capable of. Mrs. Twiggs was a very powerful Wiccan, more powerful than I had ever met. And Albert knew with that power came risk. For Albert would have given his life for her when he was alive, and now he watched over her with even more to lose. Black magic could extinguish his true light, sending him to an eternity of nothingness, but Albert stood fast in death as he did in life. His beloved Beatrice would come to no harm on his watch. Pixel glanced up, staring at the chair. It stopped rocking. He looked at me, pulling back his orange pointy ears. He flipped onto his back and fell asleep.

Mrs. Twiggs's gentle snoring sung me into slumber.

I knew I was dreaming. We can move between dreams in and out of the waking world. Because Elizabeth is standing in front of me, I knew it was a dream. I had spent the past centuries searching for her only to catch a glimpse of her in the waking world. In my dreams she stepped into my memories. I was dreaming of May Day in Salem before the secret was told. Elizabeth was warning my coven, "Hide well your cheer, my sisters. Hide your folly and your young girl's nonsense. May Day is a time of great celebration and hope, but also it brings with it great risk. Do not expose yourself. The humans forbid this celebration and will not look kindly on your dancing nor any other frivolity."

We sat under the great oak on the outskirts of Salem Town. I could feel the grass between my fingers… fingers. I have not felt fingers in three hundred years. I smelled Elizabeth's perfume of peonies and gardenia.

Sitting next to me, Prudence whispered, "We're meeting in the woods tonight as the clock strikes midnight and the May Day arrives. We will greet it with song and dance."

"Prudence, have you not heard a word that Elizabeth has spoken?"

"Elizabeth won't find out. I've spoken with the others. They agree. Elizabeth worries too much of her reputation and her fiancé."

I knew better than to try to convince Prudence of anything. She was as stubborn as she was powerful. It was she who should have been the witch's apprentice not I, but neither one of us questioned Elizabeth as she had chosen me. Her bloodline ran too deep to be challenged.

"Prudence," Elizabeth scolded.

Prudence turned to attention.

"Do I distract you?"

"No, of course not, Elizabeth. I'm sorry."

As I gazed at my sisters, my heart ached, knowing the fate that awaited them. Unlike them, I would remain in this world but not in my true form. Elizabeth waved her hands, signaling the meeting was adjourned. I wanted to tell her what Prudence had told me, but I couldn't. Cat got your tongue? I scolded my dream self. As the night approached, I found myself in the woods. I could see the other lanterns darting through the thickets like playful fireflies as my sisters gathered in the clearing at the far side of Master Johnson's farm. Prudence was wearing daisies in her long dark hair. She lifted her skirt to reveal her silver buckles to me that reflected the moonlight. She smiled with her beautiful Prudence smile. I thought how much I loved her, more than even the others. We had been more than best friends since childhood. She was my confidante and my true sister. Though not by blood but by love and circumstance. We all joined hands and completed the circle as we danced under the full moon.

Prudence led the choir in song. "Bring this day, bring this day a new plentiful harvest. Come this May to bring us joy. Your flowers and promises we rejoice in."

We danced until I was dizzy, and we all fell to the ground, laughing. I stared up at the stars. I could name the constellations, both the human and the witch stars. Like our spirit trees, witches have their own star. Mine was in the constellation Orion. Elizabeth had traveled to her star or so she had told me. I never knew if that was the truth or a story she told to excite a young girl's imagination.

Prudence reached into her cloak and retrieved a leather pouch. She whispered, "Hogweed from a shallow grave."

I shook my head. "No, Prudence."

The buzzing grew louder. When I woke, Mrs. Twiggs was levitating over her bed, her eyes wide-open and milky white. It was three a.m. "Terra, it's Mrs. Lund. She needs us to come to the Biltmore immediately."

A BODY IN
THE BILTMORE

I FOLLOWED MRS. TWIGGS INTO THE basement of the Biltmore through the Halloween room, its garishly painted stone
walls casting an eerie glow. When not filled with tourists, the dimly
lit corridors echoed. The urgency of the premonition made Mrs.
Twiggs hurry through the corridor. The Edison bulbs overhead
flickered. This part of the Biltmore Estate had not been updated.
Even without my acute cat senses, I would have smelled the sul-
fur. A rush of cold air blew past me. I could feel a presence. Even
ghosts have an aura around them. This presence had no light, no
color, no presence. Or maybe it was my imagination.

"Me scared, Terra." Pixel clung to my back.

"It's okay, Pixel."

Mrs. Twiggs took the skeleton key from her pocket. She jiggled
it in the door lock. "It's not opening, Terra." Mrs. Twiggs placed
both her hands on the old oak door. She took a piece of chalk
from her sundress pocket and drew a doorknob above the existing
one. She whispered the incantation I had taught her, and then she

twisted the chalk doorknob. The door crept open with a moan. Mrs. Twiggs lit her flashlight, shining it around the storage room. In the heart of the room, two mannequins stood in Confederate gray uniforms, the third lay on top of Mrs. Lund with an outstretched arm brandishing a Confederate saber thrust through her heart.

Mrs. Twiggs gasped, taking a step back.

DETECTIVE WILLOWS,
I PRESUME

WE STOOD OUTSIDE AS WE waited for the detective to finish his preliminary investigation. The large man in an ill-fitting brown suit brandishing a detective's badge, Detective Willows, came out, peeling off his gloves. "And what were you doing here this late at night?" Detective Willows asked Mrs. Twiggs.

"I had a feeling."

"What do you mean?"

"A premonition."

"About Mrs. Lund?"

"Yes." Mrs. Twiggs slid down to the ground, out cold. She had fainted. I stepped close to her mouth, pushing my breath into hers.

Detective Willows lifted her up and carried her into the nearby kitchen. He placed her on a chair. "Mrs. Twiggs, Mrs. Twiggs?" He caressed her cheeks, trying to rouse her. "Mrs. Twiggs. Mrs. Twiggs," the detective repeated.

She opened her eyes with a flutter. "What happened?"

"You fainted."

Mrs. Twiggs gazed around the kitchen and realized the detective had carried her in. Her face turned a bright red.

I've known Detective Willows for years, as he is a frequent visitor of the Leaf & Page. He is a kind man. A forty-year veteran of the Asheville police department. His wife had begged him for years to retire, but he couldn't. He loved his job and the people he protected. After his wife died, Detective Willows decided it was time to retire. Until he received the call about the body in the Biltmore.

He smiled at Mrs. Twiggs, which made her blush even more. "Let's get you a cup of tea and then we can talk."

I watched Mrs. Twiggs's aura change colors. She had become quite close to Detective Willows since his wife's passing. Detective Willows held the delicate teacup and saucer; they looked like a child's play set in his large hands. He carried his girth with ease and grace. For a man of his size, he was a remarkable dancer, having won many dance contests at the annual Asheville dance competition.

"Beatrice, take a sip."

Mrs. Twiggs sipped slowly, her eyes popping open at the first taste.

"I've fortified it."

Mrs. Twiggs finished the tea.

"Beatrice, there must be some reason aside from your premonition that you were here today. It doesn't sound good. Premonition? Vision?" Detective Willows shared the skepticism that many police officers felt for mystical events in Asheville.

"Butch, I've always had a sense of foreshadowing, but it's been stronger as of late. I can't explain it. I see things before they happen."

"Next time you see something, call me first. We'll keep it between us. Let's get you home. We can discuss this more tomorrow."

Detective Willows helped Mrs. Twiggs up, leading her to the door. EMTs carried the body, Mrs. Lund, out on a gurney as police investigators roped off the room with yellow caution tape. I stayed close to Mrs. Twiggs, lost in my thoughts. Why would someone want to harm Mrs. Lund? Who was she? We knew little about her. All we knew is that she was a known Civil War expert from the University of Richmond in Virginia and that she was dead.

A TWITCH OF THE NOSE

IT WAS ALMOST DAWN WHEN Mrs. Twiggs and I made it back to the Leaf & Page where Abigail and Tracker were waiting. We found them in the kitchen, which showed battle scars of white flour and yellow eggs.

"Sorry, I got into a fight with the mixer," Abigail said, taking off her batter-stained apron. She appeared as if she had lost the battle. "But I got the scones in the oven. I followed your recipe exactly, Mrs. Twiggs."

Pixel bounded into the kitchen. "Mm. Me smell blueberry." He gave a sigh of relief. All was right in Pixel's world. He leaped onto the kitchen counter to make sure Abigail hadn't forgotten any ingredients.

"You don't look so good," Abigail said to Mrs. Twiggs, who sank down at the kitchen table, her head in her hands.

"I'm fine, dear."

"Where have you been?" Abigail placed a teacup in front of Mrs.

Twiggs.

"There's been some trouble at the Biltmore." Mrs. Twiggs paused. "Actually, there's been a tragedy. Mrs. Lund is dead."

"The woman from Richmond University? The woman you met yesterday?"

"Yes."

"What happened?" Abigail asked, sitting down across from Mrs. Twiggs.

"I had a premonition she was in grave danger. It told me to go to the storage room." Mrs. Twiggs teared up. She took a lace handkerchief from her sundress pocket and dabbed her eyes. "We found her dead, a sword through her heart." And then she started to cry, her shoulders shaking.

I leaped onto the table, rubbing against her and purring. "Mrs. Twiggs, it's okay."

"I could have saved her, Terra, maybe if I would have called the police first or gotten there quicker."

"Mrs. Twiggs, she was gone before your premonition was over."

"How do you know, Terra? How do you know that?"

"You haven't learned yet how to read your visions. The stronger you get, the further in the future you will be able to see."

"I felt I was in that room with her, Terra, when she passed."

"She reached out to you, Mrs. Twiggs, as she turned from this world to the next."

After pulling the scones out of the oven, Abigail sat back down across from Mrs. Twiggs. "Don't worry, Mrs. Twiggs. I've got everything ready for today's opening." She paused and then said, "By the way, Charlotte's sleeping upstairs in the extra bedroom."

"Why? What happened?" Mrs. Twiggs asked.

"She got into a fight with Miss Hartwell and stormed out of the house. She doesn't know anyone else, so she came here."

"Oh dear, that's a shame. What could they have fought about?"

Abigail shrugged. "She didn't really say. I think she wanted to be around someone her own age. We watched a movie, hung out, and I told her to stay over."

I ran up the stairs to the second floor until I reached the bedroom. I knocked my head against the door. It was locked. I crouched down to peer under the door but couldn't see anything from that vantage point. I smelled Charlotte or at least the scent she left. I knocked on the door gently, and then I knocked louder. I don't know why I felt the need to check to make sure she was in her bed and safe. When she didn't answer, I shook off the feeling and returned to the kitchen in time to hear Pixel say, "Me help." He pulled his paw back from the hot scones.

"It's time to open the shop. Thanks for all your help, dear." Mrs. Twiggs smiled at Abigail and then went into the front room where she walked over to the picture of Albert. She raised her fingers to her lips, kissed them, and then held her fingers to his lips. He smiled down at her as she opened the front door. She greeted each customer warmly and many of them with a hug while Abigail took orders for morning tea. Mrs. Twiggs maintained her pleasant spirits during the morning rush, but I could tell Mrs. Lund's death was on her mind.

Around lunchtime, Mrs. Loblolly strolled in, wearing a bright daisy sundress. Lately I had noticed all the ladies of the Biltmore Society dressing similarly. They were donned in bright sundresses, flowered hats, and kitten-heeled sandals. Then I remembered it was late April, almost May Day. The ladies were preparing for the Wiccan holiday.

Mrs. Loblolly hugged Mrs. Twiggs. "How are you, Beatrice? I'm so excited." She looked around the room and then appeared disappointed. "I don't see her."

"Whom are you talking about, June?"

"Mrs. Lund. I was to meet her here to talk about my family history during the Civil War." She held up a family bible. "I brought our history with me."

"Oh, June, I didn't know." The teacup in Mrs. Twiggs's hand shook.

"What are you stammering on about, Beatrice?"

"Come by the fire." They sat in the wing-back chairs on either side of the marble-encased fireplace. "Mrs. Lund is dead."

"Beatrice, what are you talking about?"

Mrs. Twiggs hesitated before saying, "She was killed in the storage room of the Biltmore. I was there last night. I saw her."

"Oh, Beatrice, this is horrible." Mrs. Loblolly reached across and took Mrs. Twiggs's hands in hers. "What happened?"

Mrs. Twiggs shook her head and pulled out her handkerchief again, dabbing at her eyes.

The silver bell over the transom tinkled in greeting as Miss Hart-well came in wearing sensible rubber shoes and an inexpensive navy-blue dress. Her mousy brown hair was tied back in a bun. The makeup she wore was applied sparingly to take away from her sunken eyes and crow's-feet. She looked worse for wear since I had last seen her. I had never seen her in such disarray.

"Miss Hartwell, thank you for coming," Mrs. Twiggs said as she rose out of the chair. She gave her a hug. "Please have some tea." Mrs. Twiggs poured her a cup.

"Thank you, Mrs. Twiggs. I wanted to check on Charlotte," Miss Hartwell said.

"Abigail, go upstairs and see if Charlotte can come down," Mrs. Twiggs said.

I followed Abigail up the stairs. Before she could knock on the door, it swung open. Charlotte stood in front of us in the same clothes she had on the day before.

"What's up?" she asked.

"Miss Hartwell is asking about you."

Charlotte sighed, shrugged, and said, "She wants me to stay at the estate. I'm not comfortable there. It's not my style."

"Come talk to her," Abigail said.

We joined Miss Hartwell, Mrs. Twiggs, and Mrs. Loblolly in the kitchen where Mrs. Twiggs had put out a tray of sandwiches. Mrs. Twiggs stared at Abigail. I wondered too how much Miss Hartwell knew of the secret of the Ladies of the Biltmore Society.

"Charlotte, I think you should come back to the estate," Miss Hartwell said. "I need your help in sorting through Mrs. Tangled-wood's things. You might want a memento."

Charlotte shrugged.

"Mr. Bridgestone, your aunt's attorney, wants to sit down with you to review the conditions of the will," Miss Hartwell added.

Abigail nudged her. "Okay," Charlotte said.

"He wants to meet early tomorrow. It's probably best if you stay at the estate," Miss Hartwell said.

Charlotte turned to Abigail with an eye roll. "Okay, fine," she said.

Mrs. Twiggs escorted them out the door and flipped the closed sign. Abigail grabbed her laptop and plopped down on the sofa in the living room. I jumped on the back of the couch. Abigail appeared to be watching a TV show. "What is this, Abigail?"

"I'm doing research. It's called *Bewitched*. I've been binge-watching it," Abigail said. "Wait, Terra, you'll like this episode. She goes back to Salem."

I was intrigued, so I snuggled down with my head on her shoulder. It did not look like the Salem I remembered. Nor did the people behave as they had in my day. We watched several episodes after that one. I was intrigued by the human portrayal of witches. Abigail twitched her nose, and a Diet Coke flew to her hand from the refrigerator.

"No, Abigail," I said. "That's not how it's done."

"Come on, Terra, lighten up."

"Who's that?" I asked.

"That's Samantha's husband, Darrin."

"He doesn't look like the Darrin from the last episode."

"There's two Darrins."

"She has two husbands?" I asked.

"No, they switched Darrins midseason."

"Oh." Television comedies made no sense to me. I'd only seen them once or twice. If the elders back in Salem Town had seen flying pictures through the air, everyone watching would have been on trial. Then a thought occurred to me. "You could learn from Samantha, Abigail. She's always getting in trouble performing magic in front of humans."

Pixel joined me on the back of the couch. "Grumpy Cat," he said.

"No, we're not watching Grumpy Cat again."

"Grumpy Cat, Terra."

"After we finish this show, okay?" Sometimes it was best to give in to Pixel.

"Okay," he said, but he was fast asleep in seconds. The last episode we watched, Samantha the witch was flying on a broom. Abigail grunted and gave me a dirty look. I let out a meow laugh and fell asleep.

PIXEL MAKES A FRIEND

Agatha Hollows Cabin,
Black Mountain

"THIS IS GOING TO WORK this time. I know it, Terra." Abigail stirred the potion boiling on the potbellied stove.

I appreciated her enthusiasm but didn't share her faith. There was only one person who could turn me back to my real self, and Elizabeth was lost to me. I had seen her twice in the past three hundred years, and the second was when she came to protect her great-granddaughter, Abigail. She had come and gone so quickly that my moment was lost. Even if she had the power to turn me back, she was in a different realm of existence. Her powers might not transfer to this world.

"Try it, Terra."

I took a sip and spit it out. The witch hazel was bitter to the tongue.

Pixel sniffed, grunted, and walked away.

"Where did you find this potion, Abigail?"

Abigail ran into the bedroom and retrieved a book. I recognized it as the one she had found under the floorboards.

"How were you able to translate that potion?"

Abigail smiled. "I placed the book up to a mirror, and the words unscrambled. I could read the directions in the mirror."

The simplest answers are usually the best. I never would have thought of that.

"It's a transformation potion Agatha Hollows used to help the dying pass from this world to the next. I thought maybe it would help you return to your true self in this world."

"Agatha used that potion to comfort the dying to reaffirm that there was a life after this one."

"Did it work?"

"No, but it provided comfort to them and their families."

Pixel's cries drew us outside. Tracker stood over the orange cat, his mouth around the cat's neck.

"Tracker, no," Abigail scolded. Pixel swatted him on the nose and took off into the woods. I chased him across the stream toward the valley, which was full of spring blooms, irises, and daffodils.

Pixel rolled about the flowers, giggling. "Tickle. Flowers tickle." He was remarkably fast for a fluffy cat.

The mountain laurels were starting to bloom pinks and whites. Pixel jumped and ran into the hollow beyond the valley. Lush green moss ran along the stream that flowed past the cabin and into the French Broad River. He stopped and stared.

"Pixel, what is it?"

"Pixel, friend." He turned his head back to gaze at me. I could see his smile as a pink-and-purple butterfly fluttered over his shoulder.

On the stream's shore bloomed fern leaf yarrow, red valerian, cosmos, rosemary, thyme, purple coneflower, pincushion scabiosa, French lavender, and heliotrope. It was a garden. Butterflies danced about, landing from one beautiful flower to another. "Butterflies are beautiful, Pixel."

"No, Pixel's friend."

"I'm sure the butterflies like you, Pixel." I hid my sarcasm. I tried not to deflate Pixel's enthusiasm.

The large purple-and-white butterfly landed on his nose. He

giggled, trying to stand still. The butterfly flew off and joined the monarchs, the silver-spotted skippers, pipevine swallowtails. Agatha Hollows never would have planted a butterfly garden. Not that she didn't appreciate their beauty, but she was a practical woman. There was no medicinal property to these flowers. This garden hadn't been planted with that purpose. We sat for hours, watching the butterflies, mesmerized by their flight and their beauty. My cat instincts screaming at me to catch one, I held back. I held all life sacred even the mice I had to eat when I was starving. I made quick of them to spare their suffering. I hated that part of my life. The more Abigail tried to change me back, the more I hated being a cat. Even the slightest hope brings despair. But I cannot resolve myself to this eternity of this creature's body. I wish I had the bliss of ignorance like Pixel. He is what he is, and that's enough for him.

"Fairy garden?" Pixel asked.

"Yes, Pixel, like the garden Mrs. Twiggs planted behind the Leaf & Page." When she arrived in Asheville, Mrs. Twiggs planted a garden for the "wee folk," complete with stone cottages, a waterfall, and twinkling lights. It was housed in the small yard behind the store. I had never met an actual fairy. Mrs. Twiggs did her best efforts to attract them to her little garden, but I knew better. They had been driven out of this world many years ago. I'd never told Mrs. Twiggs. She enjoyed her fairy garden and her fairy tales.

We returned to the cabin as the sun was setting. Pixel rushed past me through the door when we smelled the turkey. Abigail's cooking skills had improved over the past few months, and the air smelled of butter and sage.

"No mice tonight," I whispered gratefully. We sat silently at the table enjoying Abigail's food.

"Terra, I think I know what went wrong with the potion," Abigail said, picking up her guitar and strumming it when we were done eating. "You're not passing through worlds, you're passing through bodies in this world."

Abigail has an inquisitive mind like all witches, a requirement to be a good witch. I didn't want to inhibit her enthusiasm. "I think you're right, Abigail. Keep looking. I'm sure you'll find a way to change me back."

Abigail smiled and handed Pixel and Tracker both another piece of turkey. She went into her bedroom and returned wearing a yellow polka-dot sundress. She twirled around as the skirt chased after her. "What do you think? For May Day?"

"You're beautiful, Abigail." She looked so much like Elizabeth, with her long white-blond hair. I remembered Elizabeth warning us about celebrating May Day, but those were different times. Ashevillians celebrated witches in a way that Salem did not. Here the witches and Wiccans were safe.

"What May Day?" Pixel asked from his spot by the fire.

"Beltane and Samhain are considered the two turning points of the year. Wiccans believe the veil between the human and supernatural world is at its thinnest, making those two days potent for magic crafting. Beltane mean fires of bel in honor of the Celtic sun god Belenus. Fire has the power to cleanse and purify. They light fires, dance, and feast."

"Feast?" Pixel's ears popped up.

"They dance around a maypole, which is a spring fertility ritual."

"Pixel like feast. Pixel like May Day." He wound around me, purring and nuzzling me.

"We're going to celebrate," Abigail said. "We'll tell the ladies."

"Yes, I believe it is safe." It would do the ladies good to have a celebration. It would be relief from the recent darkness.

"What do you mean safe, Terra?"

"I've seen a lot of magic awakening in Asheville. Celebrating May Day would draw that magic out. We need to control it before it is commanded elsewhere and becomes black magic. We need to find a ninth Wiccan to complete the circle. This could draw her to us."

Abigail half listened as she admired her reflection in a copper kettle. I hadn't thought it possible, but she was becoming more beautiful. Bryson stared at Abigail as she stared at herself. Watchers had deep affections for their watched but never turned that into love. That was dangerous. Bryson loved Abigail. He saw me staring at him and disappeared.

TRAINING DAY

"RIGHT ON TIME," I SAID to Abigail as she opened the cabin door. Mrs. Raintree stood on the porch, dressed in an authentic Cherokee medicine woman's dress and hiking boots. Her dark brown eyes sparkled in the morning sun; her long raven hair with its single silver streak was braided down her back.

"You are taking this seriously, aren't you?" Abigail asked.

"Of course, Abigail. This dress is almost two hundred years old. It's older than the Trail of Tears. It's been passed down to the women in my family. I've never had an occasion to wear it."

Abigail gathered a backpack. She had filled it with beef jerky, trail mix, and bottles of water, none of which we would need for our adventure, the purpose being to teach both Mrs. Raintree and Abigail how to survive in the woods. We headed out down toward the valley, making our way along the ridge that ran halfway up Black Mountain. Pixel and Tracker stayed close to us even while they ran off to chase butterflies. I led the way. We stopped under a willow tree along the stream. Mrs. Raintree bent down, cupped her hand, and took a drink from the stream. Abigail ran her hand along the bark of the willow tree and pulled it away, leaving her hand full of sticky sap.

I walked up to Abigail. "Gather mud from the stream bank, Abigail," I told her. She did as I requested, scooping it into the metal pail she had brought with her. "Cover your hands and arms with the mud."

"Why, Terra?"

Mrs. Raintree watched intensely. "There are dark creatures that hunt at night, not by sight but track you by the heat radiating off your body. They track you by your colors. The mud will contain your body heat."

"You mean like in *Predator*?"

I didn't understand the reference. "Yes, predators hunt at night, Abigail."

"You don't mean like vampires, do you?" Mrs. Raintree asked.

"No, vampires aren't real."

Mrs. Raintree walked in front of me. I studied her gait. "Mrs. Raintree, stop a minute. Put your fingers in your ears."

She looked at me with a question mark.

"Please," I repeated. "And then start walking."

She did as I asked. I ran up to her and stopped her by placing a paw on her leg. She removed her fingers. "Could you hear the thud of your steps as you were walking?" I asked.

"Yes, Terra."

"That's the sound of wasted energy, traveling through your knees and feet into the ground. You are burning extra calories and creating extra impact on your joints, and you're making it easy for hunters to find you. Now take your boots off. Try walking now. Notice the impact of the ground is closer to the front of your foot. I want you to land your forefoot first. This impact is absorbed by your body's natural shock absorber—your forefoot instead of the heel. You see how much quieter you walk now."

Mrs. Raintree reached into her backpack and removed a pair of moccasins. I nodded. "Those will mimic your bare feet."

We walked for several miles, stopping in a small clearing surrounded by early spring purple phlox and yellow lady slippers. I stared up at the clouds. "Thin, wispy clouds up high," I said. "If they are still, it means good weather for at least the next day. If they move quickly, it means a change is coming. If those clouds blanket the sky so thin that they give the sun a halo, that means a storm is coming soon. Gray clouds you can expect rain before the end of day. If those gray clouds form at a lower elevation and build becoming thick, that means thunderstorms by afternoon. If that gray blanket is low and has a constant drizzle, there will be no thunder or lightning. Most importantly—" I looked over at Abigail picking flowers. "Abigail," I yelled.

She snapped her head around.

"Most importantly I was saying, low-lying thunderheads with an anvil top. If these puffy clouds get taller, head for shelter."

"Terra." Abigail waved her finger in the air, making a swirling motion. The clouds drifted into a funnel cloud.

"Where did you learn that, Abigail?"

"In one of the hundreds of books you made me read."

Before I could stop her, lightning struck a tall pine, slicing it in two. Pixel and Tracker ran. A heavy limb fell inches from Abigail's head as she fell to the ground, covering herself. As quickly as it came, the funnel cloud disappeared.

I leaped on top of Abigail. "Stupid girl, you could have died."

Her eyes turned bright blood red. For the first time, I feared her. In a second her eyes turned back to violet.

"I'm sorry, Abigail, I didn't mean to say that. Even the most powerful of witches is a slave to nature. We can suggest to her how to act, but we can't totally control her." I stopped. "Lesson learned. This is why you have to learn to live with nature."

We reached a branch of the French Broad River, unique because it is one of the only rivers that flows north. I pointed out the deep bend. "Never cross here. The near bend will be calm and shallow while the outside of the bend will be deeper with faster water that you won't see. And never cross a fast-moving river that is as deep as your chest."

We walked along the river, following a stream that branched off toward the deep woods until we reached a springhead. "This water is safe to drink coming from the ground deep inside the mountains. The cleanest springs emerge from vertical ground either a stone face or earth. If you don't have a stream to follow, follow a dry creek bed. It will lead you to clean, fresh water. Follow it up the mountain as high as you can and then dig two to three feet down, and you will find water."

We stopped by a rotting log. Tracker stuck his nose in it. Pixel leaped onto it. I reached down with a claw, pulling out a paw full of termites, eating them quickly. Abigail winced. Tracker and Pixel mimicked me. Tracker spit them out. Pixel scooped another pawful. "There's more nutrition in an ounce of termites than in a steak."

We followed the stream to where it entered a cave. I felt the ancient magic emanating from deep within the mountain. "Do you feel that, Mrs. Raintree?" I asked.

She placed her hand on the cool, damp wall inside the cave. "I feel something, Terra. It feels like a low electrical current. What is that?"

"Black and white witches leave behind a trail of magic. Think of it like Hansel and Gretel leaving crumbs behind to find their way home. If you know how to follow those crumbs, it will lead you to their magic."

"Cool. Like a scavenger hunt," Abigail said.

"Of sorts," I acknowledged. "You can gather that magic, but be careful to leave the black magic that was left to confuse and harm you."

"How do you know the difference?" Mrs. Raintree asked.

"The current that you feel is in tune with your inherent magic. Do you feel how that current flows into you from the wall through you and back, completing the circuit?"

"I feel tingly all over."

"Feel your pulse."

She stood quiet and placed a hand on her wrist. "It's steady and slow."

"That means it was left by a white witch. If it were left by black magic, your body would try to resist it; your heart would beat quickly and irregularly. A fight-or-flight chemical reaction," I said.

We journeyed farther into the cave. Abigail ran her hand along the wall, causing the granite to glow with a soft light. A vein of that white light chased us along the wall as we walked until we reached the great cavern. Overhead the stalactites dripped with water and limestone. "Careful," I said, "Don't wake the bats."

"Not vampire bats?" Mrs. Raintree said.

We crouched on a ledge, listening to the babble of the water. "You've been here before, haven't you, Terra?"

"Yes, Agatha Hollows brought me here when I first came to Asheville."

Abigail looked around the cavern. The walls were covered in Cherokee drawings. Mrs. Raintree read to us. "This is a holy place, Terra. Only the medicine men and women were allowed here." She walked to one of the drawings. It was a picture depicting what the humans called an angel floating over the mountains with one wing broken. "This is Agatha Hollows, isn't it?"

"Yes," I said. "She was a fallen angel, wounded in the ancient war. What the humans call an angel, what witches call one of the old ones, an earth walker. She came down from her star to regain her strength and hide from her enemies."

"The cries of my people brought her to rescue us, didn't it?" Mrs. Raintree asked. She understood the heavens hold many mysteries.

"Yes," I said.

Mrs. Raintree traced her fingers along the drawing. Her body shook. "I can feel her. This was her magic?"

"Yes, she left a trail for us to follow."

Mrs. Raintree sang a Cherokee song for us, a melody I had heard at the cabin, a melody older than the mountain we sat under. "We'll be safe here tonight," I said when she was done. "Sleep. This mountain is a dream catcher. Open up your mind and your hearts to it." I heard a splash. Pixel had tumbled into the stream, trying to catch a fish.

He mumbled, cursing a cat curse as water spewed from his mouth. He shook his fur. "Pixel no like."

Abigail snapped her fingers and lit a fire for Pixel to dry his fur. He rubbed against her. "Pixel, you're all wet," she scolded. Abigail shared her beef jerky with Pixel and Tracker.

Mrs. Raintree sang us to sleep as I caught my dream.

"My star?"

"Yes, Terra, on Orion's belt, see, at the bottom." Elizabeth pointed up at the Salem night sky. As she stared up, I stared at her. She was seventeen years just weeks from her spirit tree birth. At eighteen years when a witch finds her spirit tree, she joins her blood to her bloodline.

"Can witches really travel to their witch star, Elizabeth?"

Elizabeth looked over with her Elizabeth smile. "Yes, Terra."

My eyes flew open, my heart pounding. I looked at the sleeping Abigail with jealousy in my heart. "That should be me," I said.

In the morning, we continued our walk out of the cave and up to the precipice of the mountain. From there we could see the hollows and the valley below. The morning sky was beautiful, blue with a red lipstick streak as the sun rose. We spent the morning identifying medicinal herbs, roots that could be used in potions, traces of witch magic left behind. Mrs. Raintree was a fast learner. She knew her family history, and more importantly, she believed in it and the power of mother earth, the source of her magic. We came to a clearing and a field of wilted irises.

"It's getting late in the season for irises." She reached down and touched one. It rejuvenated to a beautiful purple. Each one she touched came alive to its early spring glory. She turned and smiled at me. "Terra, I dreamed last night about the hunters. The ones that were tracking Agatha Hollows. I felt their magic in the cave walls also. They are still hunting her."

Abigail turned her gaze. "What is she talking about, Terra?"

TANGLEDWOOD
ESTATE SALE

E MMA TANGLEDWOOD'S ESTATE WAS SUBSTANTIAL. In
size, it was slightly smaller than the Biltmore, but it nearly
matched it in grandeur and elegance. The line had started early,
reaching out to the long line of poplars that stood on either side
of the driveway. Today was the estate sale, and all the ladies were on
hand to ensure success. Sitting in the grand foyer, Charlotte mon-
itored people filtering through the massive door, imported from
a French cathedral, an example of the exquisite taste and limitless
wealth of the Tangledwoods. There had been talk about the Tangledwoods' wealth and how it had been made. Some said cotton,
others tobacco, no one seemed sure. Mrs. Tangledwood's many
collections did not convey the taste of the frugal woman I knew
her to be. She was wont to save a penny where a penny could be
saved, but in turn she had an eye for beauty and quality wares. She
had spent thousands at the Leaf & Page with Mrs. Twiggs's help,

hunting down first editions and other rare books on magic and the occult.

Due to her status, the sale was by invitation only meant for only the elite of Asheville with all proceeds being donated to the Biltmore Preservation Foundation. Its past president now also passed, Emma Tangledwood had wanted her beloved collections to stay in Asheville. Mrs. Twiggs walked through each room, sharing information with buyers about the antiques, their values, and their provenance. The rest of the ladies rang up sales, answered questions, and wrapped valuable purchases. Abigail came into the foyer, sitting down next to Charlotte while I enjoyed the sun sneaking in from the stained-glass sidelights.

"Charlotte, how are you doing?" Abigail asked. "It's been a lot, huh?"

"Yes, it has."

"What about the rest of your family? Your parents? Are they coming here?"

"My parents are dead, and even if they were alive, they wouldn't have come anyway. My aunt wrote them out of her will… bad blood," Charlotte said.

Abigail frowned. I could see the pain in her eyes, pain for her own loss. Abigail's parents had been lost in the floods following Hurricane Katrina. She moved closer to Charlotte. Emma Tangledwood had not been the easiest person to get along with. She had a remarkable passion for philanthropy but strong opinions that she shared with everyone. Although some had been turned off by her prickly exterior, I had appreciated it.

"You look like you could use a little fun," Abigail said.

Charlotte smiled. Abigail pulled Charlotte out of the house. They walked to the end of the crowded long driveway. When the estate had disappeared behind them, Abigail said, "Wait here for a second." Abigail ran behind the trees, not knowing I was behind her. She closed her eyes and whispered an incantation. The roots of the poplars danced around the ground like delicate fingers, clasped together, picking up dirt and grass molding the shape until it became a motorcycle. Abigail turned and beamed with great pride. "It's a 1966 Triumph, 750 like my dad had. I pictured it in my mind." She jumped on the bike, started it, and drove to the road where Charlotte was waiting. "Get on."

Charlotte jumped behind Abigail and put her arms around her waist. She took off, leaving me in the dust. Abigail's youth betrayed her. She put us all at risk, performing magic like that so close to a human. I would have to caution her when she returned.

I headed back to the estate sale. Mrs. Twiggs greeted me at the front door. "Where is Charlotte? I need her help."

I stuttered. "She… she… she and Abigail took off."

"Took off? What do you mean?"

I had no answer.

"Never mind." I sensed Mrs. Twiggs shared my frustration with Abigail. "There's a man here asking about one of Emma's paintings, but it's not on the sale list. He's not on the invitation list either. In her will, Emma specifically stated that the painting should go to Charlotte. It's locked away with the other Not For Sale items."

Intrigued I followed Mrs. Twiggs to the sitting room where an older man with white hair and white beard sat in a cigar chair. He was elegantly dressed in a three-piece suit and tie.

"I'm sorry," Mrs. Twiggs said, pausing to look at the man.

He rose out of the chair and said, "I'm Darren White."

"Yes, of course, so sorry, Mr. White. I couldn't find Charlotte. I'm afraid we can't sell the painting without checking with her."

"Can I at least see the painting? I deal in antiques of the Van-derbilts. I understand that Mrs. Tangledwood shared my interest." He had an air of old-world gentility and spoke with a Southern charm.

She thought for a moment. "Let me go get it." Mrs. Twiggs left and came back a few minutes later, carrying a large oil painting depicting a field of flowers leading to a stone bridge. She placed it against the wall.

He studied it, hands clasped behind his back. He leaned down and examined the signature with a jeweler's loupe. "It's definitely authentic. It's a very important piece. Are you sure it's not for sale?"

"I can't sell it without consulting with Charlotte, and she's not here."

"Ma'am, that's a shame. I've come a long way. What can I do to convince you?"

"Really there's nothing I can do," Mrs. Twiggs said. His South-ern charm turned sour.

An awkward moment passed as if he was refusing to leave. "Here is my number if she returns and is willing to sell it." He handed Mrs. Twiggs a card before turning quickly. "Thank you for your time." Then he left the room.

I felt a peculiar twinge as he brushed past me. I couldn't recall where I had felt it before, but it gave me a sense of foreboding. I brushed it off. Maybe it was simply my cat intuition.

The day flew past, sales brisk, lines of shoppers until the sun started to set. After the last customer had left, the ladies settled in the sitting room. The front door burst open, and Charlotte and Abigail wandered in, giggling.

"You both look like something the cat dragged in," Mrs. Stickman said, eying them. Their hair was windblown, their faces weather-burned, and their smiles lopsided.

I knocked into Mrs. Stickman, resenting her comment. I knew it was a common expression, but I didn't appreciate it.

"Doris, why don't we all go into the kitchen and I'll make some tea? It's been a long day. Apparently longer for some." Mrs. Twiggs ran a pointed eye over Charlotte and Abigail. Abigail attempted to straighten her hair.

The ladies gathered around the enormous marble island. Mrs. Twiggs ran her hand along the cool marble and let out a deep breath. She missed her old friend.

Mrs. Stickman sat across from the two girls. "Have you two been into some mischief?"

"I've been showing Charlotte around Asheville," Abigail said.

Charlotte smirked.

I couldn't draw my gaze away from Charlotte. The sense of foreboding that I had earlier had returned. There was something about Mr. White that gnawed at me in the same way that Pixel was now gnawing the last of the cherry tarts. He reached up the back of Mrs. Twiggs's leg, begging for more. She had a soft spot for Pixel and obliged him. I yawned and tried to catch a catnap with one eye left open.

Mrs. Stickman shivered, stood up, and peered out the kitchen window at the distant Blue Ridge Mountains. Lightning struck across the peak. She whispered, "It's fixing to storm."

Mrs. Twiggs set out teacups and poured us her special brew.

Mrs. Stickman examined the teacup. "These are Emma's antique Wedgewood." She read the bottom of the teacup. "Floral Eden."

She set it down. "For a practical woman who counted her pennies, Emma always had exquisite taste."

Miss Hartwell came into the kitchen, wiping her hands on a dust towel. "I think Mrs. Tangledwood would have been happy with the sale, don't you think?"

Mrs. Twiggs nodded and poured Miss Hartwell a cup of tea. She sat across from Mrs. Twiggs. "The auction company will be here tomorrow to pick up everything that didn't sell today. Mr. Bridgestone, the attorney, called. He'd like to see you, Charlotte, in his office tomorrow to discuss your aunt's estate."

Charlotte smiled and sipped her tea.

"Beatrice, tell me where you get this tea. It's heavenly," she said.

Mrs. Twiggs cupped her teacup. "Abigail, speaking of tea. I spoke with Mrs. Owen about that herb you were searching for. She's going to check with her supplier."

Abigail nodded, adding more sugar to her tea.

"Squirrel?" Pixel muttered, lifting his head up. Squirrel was Mrs. Owen's familiar—a black-and-white tabby that Pixel was fascinated with. Charlotte reached down and patted Pixel's head, not understanding his cat noises.

Mrs. Twiggs pulled cash and a ledger out of her apron pocket.

Charlotte whispered, "How'd she die?"

Mrs. Twiggs shuddered and placed her teacup on the saucer with a loud clink. A gentle rain began, drops splatting against the kitchen window. Mrs. Stickman wiped her eyes with a handkerchief. I nudged her.

"I mean I know she was very old," Charlotte said. "No one said."

"Emma had a very large heart. She was a very giving, loving friend, and that heart gave out," Mrs. Twiggs said.

A light danced onto the table. I resisted the urge to chase it.

"Light, Terra." Pixel bit my ear. "Chase light."

From the corner of my eye, I saw Charlotte running a laser light along the wall. Pixel chased it up and down. Not being able to resist, I joined the chase. Charlotte and Abigail laughed.

A FAIRY RING

NOW THAT THE LEAF & Page had reopened and was fit for business, Abigail, Pixel, Tracker, and I returned to the cabin. It gave me time to train Abigail and time for Agatha Hollows's magic to assimilate into Abigail's magic. I preferred the peaceful quiet of the cabin to that of the bustle of the village. In earnest, I felt I couldn't trust Abigail to hide her magic from the humans. Abigail grabbed a basket and opened the front door. We were planning to gather herbs. She went to step over the threshold— I stopped her when I heard the telltale rattle. A large brown-and-black timber rattler was curled up on the wood porch. We froze, then Abigail reached for the walking stick next to the door. She lifted it.

"No, Abigail," I said.

"I can kill it, Terra," she said.

"Slowly back into the cabin and close the door," I said, keeping my eyes on the pit viper. Abigail did as I told her.

"I could have killed it, Terra," she said.

"Yes, but if you had, its mate and offspring would come back and take its vengeance. It will leave on its own," I told her. "Count the number of rings on its rattle."

"Five," Abigail said as she stared out the window.

"That's the number of times that rattler has shed its skin, meaning that it could have up to twenty offspring. That's a lot to haunt us, Abigail."

We waited for the snake to uncoil itself and slither away. After it left, we headed outside, this time with Pixel tagging along. We followed the stream, searching for herbs essential to our potion.

"Abigail, wait a moment." I pointed out a tall green plant with bright orange-and-red flowers growing along the bank. "Abigail, this is jewelweed or wild impatience. It contains a natural soaplike chemical. Its scientific name is saponin. It works like an anti-inflammatory. When you apply the juice of the flower on your skin, it's good for mosquito bites, chigger bites, and even poison ivy."

As we strolled, I pointed out many of the plants that Agatha Hollows had shown me. "This unassuming green weed is called broadleaf plantain. It's also good for insect bites. It grows everywhere." I saw some yellowroot, growing along some rocks. "Abigail, you see this leaf, it's triangular with feathered edges."

"Yes, Terra."

"It's called yellowroot and is good for upset stomachs. It releases a chemical called berberine. It helps with mouth sores and bacteria." I kept looking while we walked. "This tree is a dogwood, Abigail. It grows all over the Carolinas. They make a tea from the inner bark to help with migraines and reduce fever. It contains a chemical called cornic acid which is similar to the chemical used in aspirin."

Pixel listened in, eager to learn. He nibbled at each plant as I taught Abigail. "Abigail, everything you need to survive you can find in these woods. You can't always count on your magic."

Abigail sat on a log. I leaped up next to her. "As powerful as you are, Abigail, there are limits to your magic. Each time you use your magic, you enter a refractory period giving your body time to recharge. The more elaborate the magic, the longer the refractory period. One day you might need to survive without your magic, you understand?"

"Of course, Terra. I survived on the street for years without using magic, just my wits and good looks," she said with a wink.

We came across the first ingredient for our potion, its white flowers pointed upward similar to a daisy. "Abigail this is blood-root. Take a pinch. It has many uses including inducing vomiting, emptying the bowels, and reducing tooth pain. However, we need it to open the blood vessels to help absorb the rest of the potion." I stopped at the next plant, a long white flowered plant that resembled a pipe cleaner. "We need a thimbleful of black cohosh. Just a thimbleful because it might upset our stomachs. It's another blood conditioner."

"I don't know what that means," Abigail said.

"The ladies used it when they were going through the change of life to help with hot flashes. It's also known as rattlerot," I said passing my knowledge onto her. We spent the rest of the day, identifying plants and herbs until we gathered all our ingredients.

"Terra, have you seen Pixel lately?"

"Come to think of it. I have not. He was with us, examining each plant." I sniffed the air but could not smell him. I was worried.

"Pixel," Abigail shouted as we traced back our steps until we heard Pixel's laughter. We followed his sounds into a clearing where we saw him running in circles. He stopped out of breath.

"Terra, come run." He caught his breath and then continued his sprint around.

"What's he doing, Terra?"

I stepped closer to him. Pixel had found a fairy ring, at least that's what the mountain folk called it. It was a large growth of mushrooms in a perfect circle at least thirty feet across. He finally exhausted his energy and plopped down in front of me. "Terra mushrooms."

Abigail knelt down and examined one of the mushrooms. "Terra, why do they grow in a circle like that?"

"Part of the fungus that grows in the ground absorbs the nutrients in the soil. This breaks down larger molecules into smaller ones. The fungus continues to move outward as it exhausts all the nutrients in the center of the circle. The center dies forming a living ring around it as the mushrooms grow farther away from the dead earth."

Abigail started to step inside the circle. I knocked into her and she stumbled. "Don't do that."

"Why not, Terra?"

"The mountain folk believed that the fairy ring was a result of pixies or witches dancing in a circle at night."

Abigail laughed. "Well, I'm a witch."

"Better not to step inside," I told her. "According to Appalachian folklore, it could be a trap."

"C'mon, a trap?" Abigail stuck one toe inside the circle to aggravate me. She began to shake as if she were possessed.

"It's not funny, Abigail. Haven't you seen enough magic to know that anything is possible?"

She pulled her foot back quickly. "I guess you're right, Terra. Better not to take chances."

As we finished talking, I saw Pixel on his hind legs, dancing in the circle. "Me fairy."

Abigail looked at me, and then she jumped in the circle, grabbing on to Pixel's front paws as if they were waltzing. Pixel couldn't stop laughing. Abigail burst into laughter. I stuck one paw in the circle and sniffed the ground. I had seen mushrooms grow like this all over the mountains. It probably was what it was—just mushrooms. I jumped in the circle and joined the dance. Tracker danced around the outside, barking.

When we got back to the cabin, Abigail started up the stairs, then stopped, searching for the rattlesnake. Thankfully it had not returned. She hurried into the kitchen and measured all the ingredients for the potion.

"Terra?" Pixel's voice was quizzical.

"Yes, Pixel."

"What you make?"

"Abigail is making a special potion for you and me."

"What for?"

"It's called a forget-me potion. It helps people not see us, rather they see us but forget we shouldn't be there."

"Be where, Terra?"

"Anywhere, Pixel, that cats shouldn't be."

"They no like cats?"

"Of course, Pixel, everyone loves cats, but if we drink this potion, we won't have to wear our emotional support animal vest."

"Me like vest."

"Yes, I know you like the vest, Pixel, but even so this will allow us to be with Abigail."

"Me love Abigail."

"We all love Abigail, Pixel."

"Terra?"

"Yes, Pixel."

"You're a good dancer," he said before swatting me. I chased him around the cabin.

MAY DAY

"TERRA, EVERY TIME I COME here I can't help but think of Bryson," Abigail said as she strung lights around the tables on the ground of the Village Green. It was here she had met her watcher, Bryson, who had met a tragic end. Now he appeared when Abigail was in danger. She had not yet learned how to summon him, but he was always watching over her as were others she was not aware of, some good, some evil.

Mrs. Loblolly and Mrs. Raintree fixed the May Day pole in the center of the ground. Pixel chased the brightly colored ribbons that hung from it. I heard his giggles. He was so easily amused. The ladies scolded him as they strung the ribbons. The lawn was immense, the interior reserved for the May Day pole. White-clad tables had been set up around the pole. A stage was erected toward the front. I could hear the strains of music as the local orchestra warmed up, and in the far corner a large tent containing food and drink tables.

"What a glorious day," Mrs. Twiggs said as she placed a cake in the center of the sweets table. She had outdone herself. The table was festooned with trays of iced cookies in bright pinks, purples, and yellows. Hundreds of flowers adorned the tables and the grounds. The sails of the large tent billowed in the breeze. People gathered, walking about the grounds. May Day had become a festive holiday in Asheville. Traditions ran deep in the Western North Carolina Mountains. The Ladies of the Biltmore Society had always been part of the celebration. This year it took on a new meaning as they were just awakening to their Wiccan powers. The coven sat before me at a long table decorated with daisies, greeting all the folks. All dressed in flowered sundresses and the sign of a true Lady of the Biltmore Society member, a festive hat. Each lady had fastened real flowers to their hats for the celebration, trying to outdo the other. There were eight ladies in all, including dear Mrs. Twiggs.

First at the table, donned in a bright orange sundress and her large sunhat piled high with daisies, sat Jean Branchworthy. A descendant of the Celtic fire goddess Aodh, she had the power to summon fire. A powerful white witch, Aodh hurled fireballs at the invading Romans. Aodh understood the alchemy of harvesting the powers of the sun. She summoned that power through her fingertips. In the short time since her turning, Mrs. Branchworthy had made great strides in harnessing her goddess mother's power. She had tucked her long black hair up into her sunhat. There had been whispers in town about the remarkable changes in all the ladies of the Biltmore Society. While their outward appearance was worn like a cloak, their endless energy gave them away. Each lady saw their true self in the mirror: young, vibrant, beautiful. Mrs. Branchworthy had much to celebrate this May Day. Restoration on her turn-of-the-century farmhouse was complete. After her husband had passed, Mrs. Branchworthy had continued the project. Her ten-acre farm in the middle of the Biltmore Forest was worth a fortune to developers, but instead of growing ten-thousand-square-foot mansions, she grew berries and cabbages and corn to stock the Asheville food pantry.

Next to Mrs. Branchworthy sat Doris Stickman. Though her African ancestors were brought to America as slaves, her bloodline went further back, deep into the Fertile Crescent to the Egyptians, past the Mesopotamians to the earth walkers, the white witches of prehuman history. Descended from the goddess Oya, Mrs. Stickman could control the wind and bring on storms. Her dark skin glistened in the warm spring sun; her white dress complemented her. She adjusted her large organza hat filled with camellias. Her long, delicate fingers adjusted each flower to make sure it was perfect. I had spent many nights at her estate, reading her first editions. My favorite was the story of Harriet Tubman. I had only seen Ms. Tubman twice, once when she was alive, the second when she wasn't.

Nupur Bartlett stood, prim and proper, elegantly dressed in a Lily Pulitzer sage-green sundress; her red velvet hat had a silver stickpin and blue forget-me-nots. A descendant of the Indian goddess Kali, Mrs. Bartlett was our warrior. After her turning, I had given her a special silver knife forged by Agatha Hollows. When wielded by Mrs. Bartlett, that knife struck fear in the heart of evil. She had not used it yet but kept it close.

Gwendolyn Birchbark, a Southern lady of distinction, one of the few women in Asheville that still spoke with a Southern drawl. An ancestor of Kuan Yin, the Chinese goddess of mercy and compassion, Mrs. Birchbark exuded calm in her pale blue silk sundress and matching hat decorated with blue starflowers. She held a very special power, which at face value might not seem as such, the power of compassion, self-sacrifice. Qualities that black magic feared. Kuan Yin gave up eternal paradise to ease the suffering of others. Mrs. Birchbark's same qualities would protect us from dark magic. She commanded the owls that surrounded her property. Owls were always a friend of the Wiccan and kept watch and brought news of danger. She was small in stature and bore the politeness of her Chinese heritage.

She chatted with Caroline Bowers, a direct descendant of the white witch Rhiannon, one of the greatest of all witch queens. Mrs. Bowers was royalty. Rhiannon could manifest dreams and desires. She used the forest fairies and nymphs to cast dreams and fulfill wishes upon the deserving. About her estate flickered many fireflies, morphed from fairies of some century. Butterflies, dragonflies, and fireflies all at one time in their genetic history were fairies. Much like the loved children's character Tinker Bell, humans had stopped believing in fairies. Now they fly about us shadows of a memory. Her multicolored sundress swirled around her, and her large linen hat was garnished with pink, lavender, and red roses.

June Loblolly, beautiful, the former model, her once golden locks now black with the silver streak the same as that of her Wiccan sisters. No one had questioned when the Biltmore ladies appeared with black hair with a silver streak, thinking it to be part of the secret society not aware that they had become their full Wiccan selves. She sat quietly, playing with her necklace, gold and amber, a gift from her Viking foremother, the Norse goddess Freya, who had sacrificed her love to obtain that necklace. Odin had cursed her to walk the earth searching for her lost love; her tears on the earth turned into gold, then into the sea and became amber. Unlike the other ladies, June did not marry into a fortune. She built her own worth through hard work and determination. In front of her were jars of her fortune, her branded jelly and preserves. Mrs. Loblolly had the power to guide, to lead others out of darkness, to lead us to the truth. Her sunlit yellow dress danced around her long legs; her hat adorned with daffodils took on a cheerful air.

At the end of the table sat Wanda Raintree. Her witch mother was the goddess Elinhino, the earth mother. One of the sisters of the trinity, Sehu was goddess of corn and Igavhinkl goddess of the sun. Mrs. Raintree had constructed dream catchers for all the ladies to prevent black magic from entering their rooms at night. She was proud of her Cherokee heritage. Her dark black hair hung long underneath her wide hat adorned with wildflowers. Her traditional sundress was red with white strips and bore the resemblance of a tear dress, the dresses that the Cherokee women made during their forced march out of North Carolina when the army forbade them scissors.

Mrs. Twiggs, Beatrice, sat at the opposite end of the long table, greeting everyone. She wore a simple purple cotton sundress, her wide brim straw hat garnished with lavender roses. It was the same hat she wore for gardening. Her turning had been the most remarkable of all the ladies. The once large woman of eighty years now moved with elegance and grace. Her sparkling eyes, her warm smile, enchanted all who had the pleasure of meeting her. She had the power of premonition. Unlike the other ladies, I could not identify her patron goddess. Since her turning, she had many premonitions but had not learned how to decipher their meanings. I had hoped Agatha Hollows's potion would bring her clarity, but without the right hogweed the potion was not complete or effective.

Detective Willows came up to Mrs. Twiggs. It was strange to see him out of his standard-issue suit. He was wearing aqua-blue Bermuda shorts, a button-down white shirt half untucked, black socks and sandals. He smiled at Mrs. Twiggs.

"Butch, I'm so glad you came," she said as she noticed him eying the cookies. She picked up the plate and presented it to him. He grabbed three or possibly four.

"You know I can't say no to your special double chocolate cookies. You've done quite the job."

"Thank you, Butch."

"Can we talk?"

"Sure." Mrs. Twiggs stood up.

I followed behind as they went into the tent; no one noticed me. Abigail's spell, the forget-me spell, appeared to be working. I was grateful I did not have to wear the itchy ESA vest.

More tables were set up inside facing a small stage for local music acts. They sat in the front row on the folding chairs. Detective Willows's chair creaked with annoyance. I sat under Mrs. Twiggs's chair.

"Now, Butch, what brings you here?" Mrs. Twiggs asked.

"We contacted the University of Richmond, trying to locate next of kin for Mrs. Lund. They have no records of a Mrs. Lund there."

"I don't understand." Mrs. Twigs shook her head. "The Biltmore hired her for the Civil War exhibit. Surely they would have checked her references."

Detective Willows finished his third cookie and cleared his throat. "Actually, there's no record anywhere of a Belinda Lund. I ran her fingerprints and images of her face through our recognition program."

"And?"

"And she doesn't exist. At least not in any known database."

My fur stood up on the back of my neck. The sense of foreboding returned.

"I don't understand. Why was she here? And why would someone kill her?"

"We're still investigating."

"What happened to your retirement?"

"Retirement. I'll retire when I'm old," he said with a laugh. "The Biltmore Estate was good to Annabelle, and it's important to Asheville."

Mrs. Twiggs smiled and placed her hand on top of his. Annabelle Willows sat a respectful four rows back. She was now part of the Biltmore Estate. As many who passed away in Asheville, she clung to the things she loved most in life. First her husband, Butch. The second being the Biltmore Estate where she had worked as a tour guide. Detective Willows couldn't retire until he felt the Biltmore and the people around it were safe, and Mrs. Willows couldn't continue on her journey until Mr. Willows completed his.

Mrs. Twiggs darted her eyes behind Mr. Willows and smiled at Annabelle, who disappeared.

"I need to speak with Mrs. Loblolly. I understand that she was partially responsible for bringing Mrs. Lund to Asheville," Detective Willows said.

With the news of Mrs. Lund, I felt an urgency to complete Agatha's premonition potion. We were in the dark to the events happening around us.

As I thought about the potion, I felt a goose walk over my grave, a phrase I had heard during my childhood. I ran outside. Off in the distance I saw him, the rocking chair man, the apparition I had seen rocking on Karen Owen's porch, opening and closing his timepiece, reminding me of the coming darkness. He stood tall and thin, dark sockets where his eyes should have been, dressed in his morning coat, his praying mantis legs stepping slowly out of the woods toward me. Karen Owen, Mrs. Owen, appeared standing over me. She reached down and whispered, "Pay him no mind."

I shuddered. Pixel flew when he saw Squirrel, the black-and-white cat. "Me friend." They ran off onto the dark green grass and tumbled chasing bees. Pixel, I believe, had a crush on the tuxedo female cat. I did not trust her, or perhaps I was jealous?

Mrs. Twiggs jumped out of her chair and ran to Mrs. Owen, embracing her. Mrs. Owen's solemn appearance turned slightly receptive, almost a smile you might say. She was dressed in a fine, very old, violent-and-polka-dot sundress and black cloak. I rubbed up against the cloak. I could not tell its origin. It was silky-looking but rough to the touch. I felt a drop rolling down my face. I was bleeding from my head where I had rubbed the cloak.

Mrs. Owen opened the cloak and reached into a deep pocket, retrieving a small leather bag that she handed to Mrs. Twiggs. Karen Owen is a witches' apothecary, a trader of teas, herbs, spices, and magic. As in any good trade, she always expects something in return. The hogweed she had just given Mrs. Twiggs had come from another time, a time before the humans. I feared its price tag.

"Beatrice, walk with me, won't you?"

Mrs. Twiggs smiled and followed Mrs. Owen up a cobblestone path heading toward the rose garden. I kept a safe pace behind. Mrs. Owen was neither black magic nor white magic. She kept a sturdy hold on each side of that line. Hers was purely business for those who could afford her wares. I remembered Elizabeth telling me one time the phrase "time to pay the piper." Mrs. Twiggs was about to pay for her dance. They sat on a granite bench facing the rows and rows of tulips. "Karen, how did you ever find this particular hogweed? I've Google searched, I've called colleagues, I've looked through spell books."

"This strain of hogweed grows in complete darkness. It only flowers once a century. Its roots are deep in the soil of a County Cork graveyard," Mrs. Owen said.

Mrs. Twiggs appeared confused.

"It was buried in a grave some five hundred years ago."

Mrs. Twiggs held out the small leather pouch.

Mrs. Owen placed her hand on top of Mrs. Twiggs. "It's okay, Beatrice. I know your purpose is for good not evil. This plant like me serves its purpose by them who wield it."

"How do I pay for such a treasure, Karen? How do you price such a rarity?"

"In time, Beatrice, in time. Your account is good with me." Mrs. Owen gave a Mona Lisa smile.

As I feared, Mrs. Twiggs was accruing a debt she would never be able to pay. I could hear the ladies calling for Mrs. Twiggs. She rose up. "Karen, I'm sorry, there's so much to do for the celebration. Of course, you'll stay, won't you?"

Mrs. Owen sat back down. "I'm sorry. I must be on my way. Give my regards to the ladies."

As Mrs. Twiggs hurried off, I leaped onto the bench next to Karen Owen. Without warning, I felt myself lifted off the bench by my scruff. The rocking chair man twisted me around until we were eye to eye. "Put her down," Mrs. Owen commanded. For a moment the rocking chair man hesitated. As he did I could see an earthworm sliding in and out of his eye socket.

"Terra Rowan, you have no power in this world anymore, and without power you have no value. You think you mentor these ladies, but what you do is bring the black magic upon them. It is drawn to you and to your Abigail. The ladies will never be safe as long as you two are near them." I knew she was right. I had no argument for her, and then for the first time since I had known her, Mrs. Owen showed a spark of kindness toward me. "I say this for your own safety too. Get to the Dark Corner."

I closed my eyes for a second. When I opened them, she was gone. I gazed up at the sky, half expecting to see her on a broom writing my name in smoke, but that was nonsense—that's not how witches fly. The broom was a symbol—a symbol of how the original earth walkers swept the earth clean of black magic. Shrill screams brought me back to earth. I followed the sound to the front lawn. As I ran to the sound, people ran the opposite way, almost trampling me. I darted in and out of legs, searching for a clearing. The sky over the maypole was dark. My head was swimming with a loud buzzing noise. I found Pixel flat on the ground, covering his ears with his paws. Tens of thousands of locusts filled the sky over the Biltmore Village green, like a whirling dervish of darkness, blocking out the sun. They descended onto the flowers decorating the tables and maypole. They were everywhere, surrounding us, covering my fur. The ladies' hats were alive with black locusts as they ran, arms flailing, swatting them away. Running into the tent, we struggled to close the tent flaps, keeping the locusts out.

Mrs. Twiggs shouted over the noise. "What's going on?"

"Mrs. Stickman," I shouted, struggling to be heard over the buzzing.

She nodded her head and raised her hands. Lightning exploded across the sky. Dark clouds gathered followed by a heavy downpour. As quickly as they came, the locusts blew away like the great dust bowl across the prairie skyline.

A WICCAN
PAJAMA PARTY

THE SUN EXTINGUISHED OVER BLACK Mountain where
we had retreated after we had cleaned up the village green. The
ladies sat around the table in the cabin. They appeared defeated,
war torn, their hats tattered. Mrs. Twiggs paced back and forth in
front of them.

Mrs. Stickman stood up. "Okay, if no one else is going to say it,
I will. What was that Biblical apocalyptic nightmare? What just
happened in downtown Biltmore Village?"

"Terra's working on that, trying to figure out where the locusts
came from and what brought them here," Mrs. Twiggs said.

"What you mean is who sent them?"

Mrs. Twiggs was silent and sat down. Then she said, "We've all
felt dark creatures stirring. Am I right?" The ladies nodded their
heads. "And we've all felt the coming of May Day and the magic
it brings forth." They all nodded their heads again. Mrs. Twiggs

continued, "For every action of white magic, there is an equal and opposite reaction of black magic. Our celebration of May Day, our first as a coven of Wiccans, drew the black magic to us. That's why it's more important now than ever that we close our ranks, hone our skills."

June Loblolly stood up. She took her hat off, flinging it on the table. "I for one am tired of being afraid of black magic. I'm not going to live my life in fear."

One by one, each lady stood and threw their hats onto the table. After throwing hers, Mrs. Twiggs smiled. "There's the spirit, ladies. There's nothing we can't overcome if we believe in ourselves."

Mrs. Bartlett pulled her silver blade out of her cloak. In a wink of an eye, she threw it across the room where it stuck deep in the wall. Abigail ran over to remove it and the spider that clung to it. She examined the spider, and then she placed it in the center of the table where it stood perfectly still. It was no larger than a half dollar, black with red eyes. The blade flew back into Mrs. Bartlett's hand. She stabbed the table in front of the spider. It cringed.

Mrs. Bartlett bent down and spoke to the creature. "I see you, and I see your kind around my house, watching. Return to the darkness and don't come back." The spider evaporated up in smoke.

"There are spies all around us, ladies," Mrs. Twiggs said. "Minions of the darkness. Tonight we celebrate the last hours of May Day. When the veil between white and black magic is at its thinnest. We will draw the white magic to us and shut out the black magic." Mrs. Twiggs filled the sherry glasses. She added a pinch of nettle leaf to each. They raised their glasses in harmony. "To all that is good," they said in unison. They drank it down and went out the door.

I stopped Abigail at the door. "What are you doing, Terra?"

"This is not for you, Abigail. This is their battle. We can't always be there to protect them." I knew that Abigail and I would be leaving and might not be coming back.

"What do you mean?" Abigail asked.

"You are not a part of the coven."

"I want to watch." Abigail and I followed the ladies to the clearing, which was surrounded by oak, ash, and thorn trees deliberately planted by Agatha Hollows. A blood-red moon hung in the sky.

We sat quietly at a respectful distance as we watched the ladies join hands in a circle. They danced in that circle for hours with the enthusiasm of children. I felt the ripple of their joy as it expanded out into the woods. I heard the creatures in the shadows that had been watching us, scream in agony and run, slither, and fly away. Abigail looked around. She heard what I heard. She saw what I was seeing. Apparitions came out of the woods. Gentle creatures being drawn to the love of the coven.

Pixel crawled up next to me. "Who they?" he said, stuttering.

"Pixel, you can see them?"

He nodded.

"Those are humans caught between worlds."

Pixel nodded, appearing to understand me. "Like Mr. Twiggs?"

At midnight the ladies finally stopped their dance and fell to the ground, staring up at the stars. I walked around to each of the ladies and pointed out their star. I had known from the moment they turned where their stars were.

It was much too late for everyone to drive home. Mrs. Twiggs arranged the cabin with hand-sewn patchwork quilts, air mattresses, and feather pillows. We lit a fire and camped out in the living room. Abigail twitched her nose and conjured pajamas for all of them. The ladies' faces glowed from the firelight. With their giggles and smiles, they resembled a troop of Girl Scouts. I knew from that minute forth no darkness could enter their circle even without the ninth Wiccan. The Ladies of the Biltmore Society had become a sisterhood of warriors.

DORIS STICKMAN

DORIS STICKMAN HAS BECOME AN enigma to me. At one time, she was a woman of physical frailty, relying on her cane for guidance but demonstrating an incredible inner strength. A passionate woman with great empathy for those around her, she cannot control her ability to summon storms and to control natural disasters. This I see as a great concern; her emotions are so deeply tied to the environment around us. A gentle tear could turn into a monsoon. An angry word into a hurricane. I did not know how much time I had left, and for that reason I chose to do what I could, to best leave the ladies. Each would have their day and their part to play, but this day belonged to Doris Stickman. We left the other ladies asleep in the cabin and stepped out into the stillness of the dawn. A morning mist rolled off the mountains, capping their blue tips, merging the peaks into the skies.

Abigail quietly closed the cabin door behind us. Pixel complained and finally gave in once I explained he needed to stay and protect the ladies. He knew I was telling a half-truth but respected my wishes. What we were about to do was too dangerous to risk his life.

Dressed in her purple African dashiki, Mrs. Stickman relied on her carved walking stick, with a cobra head made of copper, to lead her up the path. We followed the path up Black Mountain until it ended. The mountain laurels twisted, locking arms, blocking our way. Abigail spoke an incantation, and their gnarled branches unraveled, parting like the Red Sea. We continued up the mountain, Mrs. Stickman never asking where we were going. She understood. After summoning the storm at Biltmore Village, she understood the powers she wielded. We reached a plateau, no more than two thousand feet above the cabin. Abigail flung her backpack to the ground, sitting down cross-legged. Mrs. Stickman sat next to her, relying on her cane to lower her down.

"Okay, Terra, are you going to explain why we're here now?" She reached into the pocket of her dashiki and pulled out a cigar, which she lit. She puffed smoke rings that flew to the sky like little clouds. She smiled and drops of rain fell from the smoke rings.

"I want you to summon lightning," I told her.

"How do I do that Terra? I was afraid at the May Day celebration, so when you told me to summon a storm I didn't have to think about it. It just came out of me."

"Your body is in tune with the elements, and your emotions can stir those elements, but I need you to be able to control them without emotion. To summon them as you please. That's why you still struggle with your frailty. You are letting them control you. Your body is deteriorating."

"How do I do that, Terra?" she repeated.

I ran up the plateau to a granite overhang. Mrs. Stickman creeped up and stood next to me. We stared down into the green fertile valley. The sky was bright blue with not a cloud to be seen. The morning mist burned off. "Think of yourself on a boat on an ocean. The waves are crashing against you. A violent storm is coming. You can't calm the waters around you. You must calm the waters inside you. Find your center."

Mrs. Stickman closed her eyes, taking deep breaths. As she did storm clouds gathered. She opened her eyes. "What's happening, Terra?"

"You are calming the waters within, taking all your emotions out of your magic. The storm is coming because you will it. You're in control of your mind and body."

Mrs. Stickman raised her walking stick in the air. Lightning struck across the sky. She raised her stick again, and lighting struck the copper cobra head. Her entire body glowed. She pointed her stick at an evergreen across from the overhang. Lightning flew from the copper cobra head and split the tree in two. She waved her hands, and the clouds blew away. She stood straight and tall.

Abigail cautiously climbed up the overhang. "That was really cool, Mrs. Stickman."

A FRIENDLY GHOST

I WAS GETTING USED TO WEARING the emotional support animal vest. Abigail's charm wore off, and there was no time to gather the necessary ingredients to cloak me again. I accepted the emotional animal vest. It was my way into places that normally would be closed to me. We sat in the grand foyer of the Biltmore Estate. Mrs. Twiggs, Abigail, Charlotte, myself, and my constant companion, Pixel. Even if Tracker had an emotional support vest, his youthful energy would have given him away. His constant pacing and whining would not be tolerated. A gentleman came over to us.

Mrs. Twiggs rose and greeted him. "Justin, so nice to see you," she said.

I recognized him from the pumpkin fest. Justin Pickering, director of events, had overseen the Biltmore special events for quite a few years now. We followed him back to his office where he sat down behind his large cherry desk after showing Mrs. Twiggs to the seat across from him. I appreciated the craftsmanship of his desk. It was late 1800s, probably a souvenir from one of George Vanderbilt's European furniture-finding trips. The palladium window behind him looked out over the east lawn. Pixel hopped out of Abigail's arms and sat on the small table, staring out the window. Mr. Pickering turned around in his chair and scratched Pixel's ears.

"Beatrice, I had our exterminators walk through the village grounds, trying to locate the source of the locusts."

I thought the source would not be found, at least not in this world.

"What a horrible catastrophe. It seems like the Biltmore curse is true. First poor Mrs. Lund and then the locusts ruining the May Day celebration."

"What curse are you talking about?" Charlotte asked.

Mrs. Twiggs realized she hadn't introduced Charlotte to Mr. Pickering. "Justin, this is Charlotte Tangledwood, Emma's great-niece."

Mr. Pickering rose and turned to Charlotte. "I am so sorry for your loss. She was a great woman and a great benefactress of the estate." He took his seat, turned to all of us, and continued, "The curse I'm referring to was cast upon the Biltmore and the neighboring village by a clairvoyant from Louisiana, Madame Claire. She came to host one of the many séances that George and Edith Vanderbilt held at the estate. While here, she stayed at the Fillmore Hotel in downtown Asheville, which was where many guests stayed while the estate was under construction. A great fire burned down the hotel, killing many of the guests including Madame Claire. On her deathbed, it was said she cursed the Vanderbilts and the Biltmore."

Abigail shifted in her chair. I stepped onto her lap. She stroked my fur, listening intently at the sound of her grandmother's name.

He continued speaking. I spoke with Abigail in her thoughts. "Terra, he's talking about my grandmother," Abigail whispered without moving her lips. "She didn't cast a curse. It was the evil that came for her and the book that cursed the Biltmore."

Mrs. Twiggs listened into our conversation while smiling and nodding at Mr. Pickering.

"Abigail let it go," I told her.

"He's talking about my grandmother. She's a white witch." Abigail held back tears for the grandmother she had only met as an apparition. We turned our attention back to Mr. Pickering. The conversation turned to Mrs. Lund.

"How did you find Mrs. Lund?" Mrs. Twiggs asked.

"She contacted us. She saw we were planning the Civil War exhibit, and she volunteered to come help."

"Did you verify her references? Did you call the university?"

"I didn't think it necessary since Mrs. Loblolly recommended her."

Abigail stood up. "If you don't mind, I'd like to show Charlotte around the estate."

Mr. Pickering said, "Of course."

Charlotte and Abigail ran off. I thought it best to remain behind and continue listening to the conversation.

"I went over all this with the police," Mr. Pickering said. "Of course, we've tried to keep it out of the papers as much as possible. For now we're calling it a tragic accident."

"Yes." Mrs. Twiggs nodded. Her attention turned back to the Civil War exhibit. "The ladies will be glad to help with the exhibit. They already have been volunteering family heirlooms, and I have an extensive knowledge of the battles fought in the Carolinas. And I would love to help you with the exhibit."

"Beatrice, that would be wonderful. Your help is always appreciated around the estate." Mr. Pickering gave her a big smile.

"If you don't mind, Justin, I'd like to take an inventory of the artifacts in the storage room so we can think about staging." Mrs. Twiggs stood up.

"Of course, please let us know if you need any help." Mr. Pickering walked her to the door.

Mrs. Twiggs thanked him. We headed down the long corridor to the back stairs down to the basement. This time I didn't feel the cold rush of air. Maybe because it was still daylight, or maybe I had been mistaken. We entered the storage room. Mrs. Twiggs took notes on her reporter's pad while she opened the boxes labeled for the exhibit. The mannequin that had embraced Mrs. Lund was standing upright at attention, next to the other two uniformed soldiers. The sword was missing from his outstretched hand. I noticed for the first time he wore a lieutenant's uniform. Though his wax face did not look familiar, his uniform did. I had seen it before. I walked around, sniffing the wool. I rubbed my scent against it. Pixel sat, not knowing what to make of my actions, so he copied me.

"Copycat," I whispered.

He smiled at me, not understanding the reference. This couldn't be the same uniform. There were many Confederate lieutenants in the Carolinas. I sniffed again, and though it was in excellent condition and well-kept, I could still smell the scent of the lieutenant who had come for Agatha Hollows at her cabin.

"Mrs. Twiggs, who donated these uniforms?"

She reached into her purse and retrieved a piece of paper. She ran her finger along the itemized list and then examined the uniform. "Most of the uniforms were donated by June. They're boxes of them."

"What about these three?"

She checked the list again. "Yes, these three were donated by June. She even has the provenance listed of all the uniforms. Their names and regiments."

"Mrs. Twiggs, what's the name of the lieutenant?"

Mrs. Twiggs ran her finger down the list, stopped, and then said, "There's no name listed."

As she spoke, I felt the cold draft. Pixel felt it too. Mrs. Twiggs would have felt it if she wasn't so fixated on the matter at hand. Cats and even some dogs, only the smartest mind you, can sense ghosts. Ghosts, they disturb the air, leaving a vacuum behind them. That vacuum causes the temperature to drop. Whoever this ghost was, it was not making itself known to us. Pixel followed behind Mrs. Twiggs as she continued her inventory. He did not seem upset or scared but instead bore a quiet confidence. It was something different about him.

"Mrs. Twiggs, I have to go," I said.

"Terra, do we need to leave?"

"Finish what you're doing. Pixel, stay here. We'll meet up at the Leaf & Page." I ran out of the room, down the hall and out of the Biltmore, past the crowds of tourists lined up by the front entrance waiting for the next tour. I ran until I reached the Fillmore Hotel. The only way to find a ghost is to ask another ghost. The only ghost who would talk to me stood on guard at the entrance of the refurbished hotel. I waited for the patrons as they came and went, garbed in their finest. Bradley stood at attention like a beefeater. He gave me a sly wink. I had not seen him since early fall. As the last patron entered, he stooped down to be closer to me.

"Young miss, so good to see you. Isn't she beautiful? What a fine job they did shining her up."

"Bradley, she looks wonderful. I wondered if I could speak with you."

"Young miss, I'm afraid it's a while before dinner."

"No, thank you. I'm fine. May we talk?" I had to be careful on how to approach the subject. Bradley didn't know he was a ghost, and now that the Fillmore was reopened so many years since the fire, a lot of the ghosts that had haunted it had left. Bradley was one of the few remaining. The night of the fire Bradley had rescued many of the guests, only to succumb to the smoke himself.

"I do have time, young miss, I'm due for a break."

We walked around to the alley. "Oh, before I forget. Lionel sends his greetings," Bradley said, striking me dumbfounded. "He stopped by looking for you."

"Bradley, has anyone else been looking for me?"

"Now that you mention it, a young man no more than a boy who had a very heavy Southern accent. He did not give his name. He said that if I were to see you I should tell you that you can find him at the Dark Corner. Of course, I have no idea what he meant. He seemed very nervous but pleasant. He seemed awfully young to be a soldier."

"Thank you, Bradley."

"Of course, young miss. I'll give your regards to Lionel if we cross ways again."

"Please do. Tell him how much I love and miss him."

"He knows, young miss," Bradley said as he stroked his pencil-thin mustache and winked.

JUNE LOBLOLLY

THE NEWEST OF THE LADIES' homes, the Loblolly house was Mrs. Loblolly's own version of San Simeon, built by her preserve empire. Reminiscent of her Viking ancestors, the brick fortress was surrounded by a wrought iron fence. At the top of the four-story home was a tower with a 360-degree viewing room designed to watch the sunset over the Blue Ridge Mountains. Mrs. Loblolly greeted us at the door, painted blue with yellow accents, a nod to her Swedish heritage. We walked in, wafting in the fragrance of the peonies, gardenias, and orchids that she had scattered around in her collection of crystal vases.

She was dressed simply in jeans and a cotton T-shirt. Around her neck, her gold necklace, a gift from her distant relative the Norse goddess Freya. We came for guidance. Freya guided Vikings to Valhalla; Mrs. Loblolly would guide us in a different direction.

"June, thank you for having us over," Mrs. Twiggs said.

Abigail, Charlotte, Pixel, and Tracker all settled in the great room. As of late, Abigail and Charlotte were attached at the hip as the humans say. Whatever mischief they had gotten into on the motorcycle had bound them as fast friends. Pixel left the circle to smell the flowers. I could hear him sneezing from across the vast room. Mrs. Twiggs and I spoke in private with Mrs. Loblolly.

"June, I'll get right to the point. Why did you recommend Mrs. Lund to the Biltmore?" Mrs. Twiggs asked.

"She contacted me a month or so ago about my great-great-grandfather, the colonel. She knew a lot about my family history and the Civil War. She told me she was a professor at the university and that she could help with the upcoming exhibit." Mrs. Loblolly settled onto her white leather couch, crossing one leg over another.

"And she told you that she would prominently display your family heirlooms in the exhibit?" Mrs. Twiggs asked.

"Yes, she did. She had heard about the exhibit, and that's what prompted her to call me. Obviously with my family being prominent Ashevillians. Beatrice, she had me fooled."

I knew that feeling well. We all believe what we want to believe. I had believed that my dear Prudence was my friend, but she betrayed my sisters and me.

"I'll be right back." Mrs. Loblolly stepped out of the room and came back carrying the cinnamon buns we had been smelling since we walked in the door and placed them on the coffee table. From another room, we heard a vase smash, shattering onto the hardwood floor. Pixel scampered back into the room, jumping onto the table and toward the cinnamon buns.

"Me sorry," Pixel said.

Abigail and Charlotte joined us. We ate in silence until the silence was broken.

"Charlotte, have you decided what you're going to do with Emma's estate?" Mrs. Loblolly asked.

"It's not my decision," Charlotte said.

"Have you consulted with the family's attorney?" Mrs. Loblolly asked.

"Yes, all of my aunt's estate except for a few personal items is being donated to the Biltmore Foundation."

"What about you?"

"When she tracked me down, Miss Hartwell told me Aunt Emma left me a small inheritance. She also told me that my aunt had been looking for me for years ever since my folks died," Charlotte said.

"Bless her heart," Mrs. Twiggs said. "What a shame that you didn't find each other."

"How much longer will you be in town?" Mrs. Loblolly asked.

Charlotte glanced at Abigail, who smiled. "I don't know. I like it here. I think I'll stay for a while and see what happens. This place is pretty awesome."

"Where are my manners? I should give you a tour." Mrs. Loblolly stood up again.

Abigail jumped up. "I can show you around."

I knew where Abigail would lead her, up to the viewing tower that was her favorite place when we visited Mrs. Loblolly. A tower made of glass with its 360-degree view. To the east were the Blue Ridge Mountains, then downtown Asheville, the Biltmore Estate, and the French Broad River. I was concerned that Abigail would tell our secret. I followed them up the spiral wood-and-steel staircase and listened in.

"You should definitely stay, Char. I think you'll really like this place. People are cool, the music, the food," Abigail said.

"Yeah, Abigail. I don't have much to go back to. What about your folks? You never said," Char said leaning against the window.

Abigail was silent. "They're dead."

"I'm so sorry."

"Well, Mrs. Twiggs, Beatrice, has taken me in, and really all the ladies have become family to me," Abigail said.

"What's the deal with the Ladies of the Biltmore Society? They look ancient, but they act like teenagers."

"Their clubs keep them young. They stay busy reading books, planning events, and gardening."

"When I was staying with Mrs. Twiggs, I happened to notice her stocking some books on the top shelf. She carried with one arm this heavy box up the ladder to the very top. I mean, I would have trouble carrying it, and she climbed a ladder holding it? Something is off, you know?"

"I…"

I meowed as loud as I could, interrupting Abigail's next sentence. Both girls turned.

"I think your cat missed you, Abigail." Charlotte picked me up by my scruff. I did not take kindly to her familiarity, so I unleashed my claws and dug into her arm. She dropped me. "What the?" She raised her hand to strike me. Abigail stopped her.

"Sorry, Char, she's temperamental."

"Where do you go when you're not at Mrs. Twiggs's? I've stopped by a couple of times, and you weren't there," Charlotte said.

Abigail glanced at me. I was busy cleaning my fur, getting Char's scent off me. "Mrs. Twiggs has a cabin on Black Mountain. She lets me crash there as long as I take care of her garden," Abigail said.

"Mrs. Twiggs is great. I appreciate her letting me stay there. I don't feel comfortable at my aunt's house. It's too big and kind of creepy. I'd love to see the cabin, get out of town a while, you know?"

Abigail smiled. "We better go back downstairs."

Mrs. Loblolly was clearing the plates when we came back downstairs. Pixel was cleaning his whiskers, purring loudly. "Me full." He rolled over so his white fluffy belly was facing up and ready for a good rub.

Mrs. Twiggs said, "Abigail, why don't you show Charlotte the garden? I want to speak to Mrs. Loblolly in private."

After they had left, I spoke first. "Mrs. Loblolly, we need your help to find out who Mrs. Lund really was and who killed her."

"I thought it was an accident. The mannequin fell over."

"You don't really believe that, do you?"

"No, I don't think I do. I think I feel responsible for her coming here, so I also feel responsible for her death. How can I help?"

"We need you to use your powers to guide us down a path to answers."

"How do I do that, Terra?"

"The spells you've been working on. The TM spells."

Mrs. Twiggs looked at me.

"Transcendental meditation." I turned back to Mrs. Loblolly. "I want you to think about Mrs. Lund while you hold your necklace."

As Mrs. Loblolly closed her eyes, all the lights in the estate went out. The large fireplace blazed to life. She clasped the gold chain with its drops of amber. The floor shook. Mrs. Loblolly opened her sapphire-blue eyes. For a moment she was not Mrs. Loblolly, she was the goddess Freya. She hunched over. I heard bones cracking

as the black Valkyrie wings burst out of her back. She levitated off
the ground, her wings flapping slowly. Pixel ran behind the couch.
She reached out her hand and pointed. We all turned to stare in
the direction she pointed.

Mrs. Twiggs said, "She is pointing south."

IN A JAM

A KNOCK ON THE DOOR BROUGHT Mrs. Loblolly crash-ing onto the hardwood floor. She dusted herself off and rushed to answer it. We heard her greeting Detective Willows and they came into the living room.

"Would you like something to drink, Detective?" Mrs. Loblolly asked as he sat in the flowered, overstuffed chair.

He sank deep into the cushion as he smiled and nodded at Mrs. Twiggs. He took out a little notepad from his shirt pocket and flipped it open. "No, thank you. I'm not interrupting something, am I?" he asked.

"No, of course not," Mrs. Loblolly said, sitting uncomfortably across from the detective, her leg shaking. I couldn't help noticing how nervous she was—not her usual calm self.

"I've spoken with Mr. Pickering at the Biltmore Estate. He told me you recommended Mrs. Lund to curate the exhibit," Detective Willows said.

"Well, yes of sorts." Mrs. Loblolly hesitated. "She actually contacted me."

"Why was that?"

"She said she had an extensive collection of letters and journals of the Carolina battles and specifically those belonging to my great-great-grandfather, the colonel's regiment."

"Did she have those papers?" Detective Willows asked.

"I never really got to meet with her. I was supposed to meet her at the Leaf & Page, and that's when Beatrice told me she was dead," Mrs. Loblolly said.

"You hadn't spoken to her before then?"

"Only the night before to confirm our meeting the next day and a few times when we arranged for her to come here."

"The night before. What time was that?" Detective Willows scribbled in his little notebook with his stubby fingers.

"I don't know. Ten o'clock maybe?" Mrs. Loblolly reached for her iPhone on the coffee table. "Do you want me to check for the exact time?"

"Detective, what are you insinuating?" Mrs. Twiggs asked.

"Nothing, just doing my job." Detective Willows paused. "Tell me about your relative. What was it about him that interested Mrs. Lund?"

"The Colonel Odysseus Loblolly," Mrs. Loblolly started.

Detective Willows interrupted her, stopped writing, and held his hand up. "You go by your maiden name?"

"Yes, I reverted after my husband passed. Because of my business I use my maiden name as the recipes have been in our family for generations."

He continued writing.

"The colonel was sent to White Hall to lead a militia against General Foster and the Union troops in December 1862," Mrs. Loblolly started, her voice soothing with its lilt.

I knew it well. The battle was also known as the battle of White Hall Ferry, held on the banks of the Neuse River. I closed my eyes and heard the clashing of blades, felt the dust stirring and the ground trembling.

"The Federals were trying to hold the Confederates in position while their main column continued toward the railroad; however, that was a decoy. According to the colonel's journals, the Union was after an ironclad ramming boat that was under construction on the north bank of the river. The boat, the CSS *Neuse*, was one of several boats being built throughout the south to break the Union naval blockade," Mrs. Loblolly said.

"And Mrs. Lund was interested in that? The contribution to the history books?" Detective Willows asked.

"She was aware of the stories about the ramming boat, but she told me that wasn't what she wanted to talk about. She was curious about when the colonel returned to Asheville." She paused. "You see, when he was wounded at White Hall, he came back to recuperate. He was shot in the leg, never quite healed right. He had a limp and had a hard time getting around. That's when he was assigned to the home guard. She told me she was researching stories about the Asheville home guard."

I could tell her some stories. I had encountered members of the Asheville home guard both by the cabin and in town.

Mrs. Twiggs interrupted. "You never mentioned that he was part of the home guard?"

Mrs. Loblolly cleared her throat, sipping her tea. "It's not something I'm proud of. It's not something I want Jean to know. She's proud of her Union relatives, heroes of Gettysburg and Bull Run."

"I see." Detective Willows adjusted his weight in the chair, sinking lower.

"The colonel spent the last part of the war hunting down deserters. He was killed by a deserter in South Carolina."

The detective closed his notebook. "You have no idea of Mrs. Lund's real name or who she was?"

Mrs. Loblolly shook her head. "No."

He kept his eye on the bottles of jam stacked on the buffet server until he couldn't hold back any longer. "I'm a big fan of the jam," he said.

"Please take some." She got up and handed him a few jars.

"Thank you." He placed them in his suit jacket, smiled at Mrs. Twiggs, and left.

When Mrs. Loblolly came back, I asked her, "Where was the colonel killed?"

"Right across the border near Traveler's Rest."

Abigail and Charlotte ran into the room with a crash, laughing.

"What's gotten into you two?"

"We've been talking and decided that I'm going to move in with Char at the Tangledwood Estate," Abigail said.

"What are you talking about?" Mrs. Twiggs asked.

"She wants to stay in Asheville, and it's a big house."

"It'd be nice to have someone stay with me," Charlotte chimed in.

Mrs. Loblolly gave a concerned look to Mrs. Twiggs. "Charlotte, be a dear and help me with these plates," she said. They picked up the tea service and carried it into the kitchen.

"Abigail, I don't think this is a good idea. What if Charlotte sees you performing magic? What about your training?" Mrs. Twiggs asked.

"Mrs. Twiggs, I can do that at the cabin. I need to be around people my age and nothing personal I love all you ladies, but I need a life."

"Abigail, your life is not your own," I said. She was meant for a greater purpose. "Take a minute to remember who you are and your bloodline. You started your journey to become a witch, and there is no turning back."

"Can't I do both? Can't I be a witch and a girl? Look at you. You're a witch and a cat."

I let out a little hiss that I couldn't hold back. "This was not of my making, Abigail Oakhaven. Your great-grandmother, my Elizabeth, imprisoned me in this body." And I continued. "You mock my pain and think yourself above your bloodline," I said with a hiss.

"Terra, that wasn't my intention. Come stay with us. You can make sure I keep on track, okay? But really? I need a break." Abigail crossed her arms across her chest.

I glanced at Mrs. Twiggs for an answer, and she had none.

"Anyway it's not up to any of you."

"Very well. Pixel and I will go with you."

Pixel woke up, stretched and muttered, "Go where?"

A SECRET REVEALED

"ET'S DO SOMETHING." CHARLOTTE FLEW down the
stairs. After visiting Mrs. Loblolly, we had moved into the
Tangledwood Estate. Miss Hartwell had the housekeeper prepare
rooms for us. Large master suites with sitting areas, soaking tubs,
and wood-burning fireplaces. I shared one with Abigail. Pixel preferred his own room; he said he needed quiet time or "no-talk
time" as he phrased it.

Abigail sat on one of the stools at the large kitchen island. "What
do you have in mind?" She spun around to ask Charlotte.

"Dance. Drink. Something. I don't want to sit in this house all
day," Charlotte said.

I was not sure how I felt about this young friend of Abigail's. She
might be a bad influence on my protégée. I had tried to get Abigail
back to the cabin, but she refused, always too busy with Charlotte.

"Okay. Okay." Abigail laughed, releasing her long white-blond
hair from its ponytail.

Charlotte grabbed Abigail by the hand and pulled her down the long hallway from the kitchen leading into the garage. She turned and smiled at Abigail as she opened the door to reveal a massive ten-car garage. Each stall held a magnificent work of art. "Well, Abigail, do we take the Porsche, the Bentley or the Rolls?"

Abigail shook her head until they reached the last car, encased in a white cover. Charlotte flung the cover off to reveal a 1961 Mercedes 190SL convertible, black with a blood-red interior.

"Good choice, Abigail. Miss Hartwell told me that was my great-uncle's car. He bought it new, the year after he married my great-aunt. I found some letters of my great-aunt's. One was from Germany when my uncle went to watch his car being built. Actually, a pretty passionate love letter."

I thought I had never seen Mrs. Tangledwood drive this car. She was a woman of means, but by no means was she extravagant. All the cars must have been her husband's idea. I could feel the energy coming off this car. For a moment I had visions of a young Mr. and Mrs. Tangledwood flying around the winding roads up the Blue Ridge Parkway. Mrs. Tangledwood laughing, her hair tied in a silk scarf. It was the first real memory I was able to discern from the Tangledwood Estate. When I walk in most houses, I am bombarded with sounds and smells and even visions. Memories are electromagnetic just like humans. They cling to the walls like scared children clutching a mother's leg. They engulf you in their emotions. Something about this car held the key to the memories of the Tangledwoods. Abigail was drawn to it too. Charlotte tossed the keys to Abigail. They jumped in, Abigail behind the driver's seat. Pixel was busy in the corner of the garage, searching for intruders of the mouse type. I summoned him with a loud meow. He flew to me, and we jumped into the tiny back seat.

"Can you drive a stick?" Charlotte asked.

"Yeah, my dad." She stopped for a minute. "My adopted dad had an old Mustang. He taught me to drive a stick."

"You never talk about your parents. You just said they were both dead. How old were you?"

"Let's not talk about that now. Let's take this baby out for a ride," Abigail said.

Charlotte nodded.

Abigail turned the key. The car roared to life. The diesel engine kicked on angrily but purred smooth and hungry. I smelled the oil and pipe tobacco. I jumped on the back of the seat, glancing around the garage as Abigail pulled out. All I saw was a puff of pipe smoke as the garage door closed behind us. Pixel stuck his head out the side, his tongue dangling like a dog. We headed through the rows of poplars down the cobblestone driveway that went on for a half mile until we reached the main entrance of Biltmore Forest, the small exclusive subdivision built on land that had once belonged to the Vanderbilts. Charlotte turned on the AM radio, sliding the dial up and down until she found a station playing classic rock. The song that came on gave me a chill because it was the song playing when Katrina washed away Abigail's parents. The Rolling Stones belted out "Gimme Shelter."

Abigail reached over, switching the station. Every station was playing "Gimme Shelter." She grabbed for the volume knob to turn it off. The radio grew louder.

"Abigail, look out," Charlotte screamed.

Abigail turned her eyes away from the radio in time to see she had missed a curve and was heading into oncoming traffic. She swiveled back and pulled over to the side of the road, gasping heavily for air.

"What's going on, Abigail?" Charlotte asked.

"You didn't hear it."

"Oh, the song. "Gimme Shelter." It's a good song."

"It was on every station."

"I think the dial is just broken. It was the same station."

I gently tapped Abigail with my paw. "You're probably right. I was shook up. I should have been watching the road."

"Let me be the navigator. You just drive."

"Let's head to the Orange Peel," Abigail said, the music hall downtown that hosted bands. "There's a band I've been wanting to see."

"How do you get in? It's twenty-one and older."

"I've got that covered." Abigail reached into her leather coat pocket. As she did, she looked at me and twitched her nose. A bad habit she had begun after her binge-watching *Bewitched*. Now she did it just to irritate me. She smiled and retrieved a driver's license, handing it to Charlotte. "I'm twenty-two, Charlotte."

"How'd you?"

"I've got connections. Don't worry about it."

We pulled up to the Orange Peel. Abigail found parking across the street, twitching her nose to pay the fee. I would have to have words with her about the judicious use of her powers. There was a line of hipsters waiting impatiently to get in. Many of them held their iPhone inches from their faces, giving them a ghostly hue. Abigail ran up to the bouncer, bypassing the line. He ushered the girls in. Pixel and I were able to sneak in. No one ever glanced down at their feet. Abigail's beauty kept all eyes on her. When she was in the room, no one else mattered.

Pixel and I walked between the legs clad with skinny jeans and short skirts, our paws sticking to the floor. Pixel stopped and licked his paws every ten steps.

Abigail and Charlotte were ushered to a special booth, left of the stage. Pixel and I jumped up onto the half circle bench, crouching under the table. Abigail rubbed my fur. Pixel popped his head up until his eyes were level with the table. Thankfully the room was dark and loud, and no one saw us. Pixel noticed the plate of nachos that the table next to us was enjoying. He stared at Abigail with his big saucer eyes. She smiled back and ordered a plate of nachos and two beers. The opening band came out, introduced themselves, and started playing what sounded like chaos to me. I could not get used to this din that was called music in this time; however, everyone else could, judging by the crowded dance floor.

After our second plate of nachos and fourth round of beers, a young man came over to the table. He was tall and good-looking, wearing a T-shirt that read ENCHANTING ALICE. He held out his hand to Charlotte. "Dance with me?"

Charlotte took his hand. Abigail had turned down several offers to dance instead choosing to get drunk. "Abigail, you're driving," I said.

"I'll put a spell on the car." She almost slurred her words.

"Still, you're not thinking clearly."

"Terra, I think I deserve to have a little fun. I don't know why you're here."

"Abigail, I heard the song too. It was playing on every station. Someone is trying to tell you something. It's a warning."

"It's not a warning, Terra. Not everything is black magic or white magic or goose bumps."

I knew better than to argue with her, but I knew I was right. And more importantly she knew I was right. Pixel lay on his back, licking the nacho cheese off his paw.

"Me full," he said, a phrase I seldom heard him say.

The waitress brought over another bottle of beer. I scratched Abigail's leg under the table.

"Stop it," she scolded me, swatting me away. Her eyes turned fire red as she spoke the words. I was flung against the back of the seat and fell to the floor. I had half a mind to leave her to her own doing, but I couldn't. Elizabeth never left me, and I had rebelled against her many times. The night of May Day in the woods with Prudence and the rest of my sisters. That night I had seen the true power of Elizabeth Oakhaven. As much as I loved her, I feared her, not that she would ever harm my sisters or me, but I feared what she could become if not for the goodness of her heart. I had that same love and fear of Abigail. She was not in control of her emotions or her magic, and those two worlds if ever were to collide would be devastating. I cleaned myself off and jumped back up, snuggling against her. She looked down, her eyes glassy and watery. "I don't feel so good, Terra."

She ran toward the back corner with me on her heels. She reached the women's washroom only to find the door locked. She pounded. She held a hand over her mouth and pounded again. This time the door flung open. We saw Charlotte on the floor with the man she had been dancing with on top of her. He was tearing at her clothes, his hand over her mouth. Abigail screamed, "No." His body lifted off Charlotte and smashed into the ceiling, arms and legs outstretched like they were tied to a whipping post. Charlotte's eyes burst open, staring straight up at him. His body shook, a rain shower of blood pouring out his nose onto Charlotte.

"Abigail, stop," I yelled. "Stop now." I couldn't stop her. In her rage, she couldn't hear me.

Charlotte grabbed Abigail and shook her. "What are you doing? What's happening?"

Abigail turned her gaze from him to her. And then they both ran out of the bathroom. They didn't stop until we had reached the car. Abigail bent over and threw up. Charlotte crouched into the grass next to the car, shaking. I didn't know what to do. I didn't know how to comfort either one of them. I slowly walked up next to Charlotte and rubbed my head against hers. She grabbed me and then threw me onto the sidewalk. Pixel charged her with claws extended.

"Stop, Pixel," I yelled. "She's scared. Leave her."

Pixel came back and cleaned my wounds.

Abigail composed herself and slowly came over to Charlotte, who looked up at her with terror in her eyes. She crawled backward on the ground. "Get away from me, you freak. What kind of monster are you?"

"Charlotte, listen." Abigail tried to calm her.

"No, I mean it, just keep away from me." Charlotte righted herself and took off down the crowded street.

Abigail started to take off after her. I stopped her. "Let her go." I nodded to Bryson who was behind Abigail, watching. He had come the minute Abigail broke down the bathroom door. He understood what I needed and flew off to follow Charlotte. "Keep her safe," I told him as he flew overhead.

"Terra, I'm sorry. I don't know what came over me," Abigail said, sinking onto the grass.

"Let me stop you there. You were drunk and out of control. You have no idea the power you wield. You must keep your senses about you."

"Yes, Terra, I see that now."

"Do you, Abigail?"

"What are we going to do about Charlotte?"

"Let me worry about that. Call an Uber. We're going to the Leaf & Page."

Abigail nodded.

DEAR PRUDENCE

ALBERT GREETED US AT THE door of the Leaf & Page. "Beatrice is asleep. You must be quiet." He let us in. I thought about asking Albert about the ghost from the Biltmore basement, but ghosts like humans associate in cliques according to time periods and the way they left the earth. Bradley had served in the Civil War, so the Biltmore ghost was drawn to him. Albert was a young ghost, heartbroken from leaving his beloved. He had no friends in the next world. He didn't quite understand yet that he was not living.

Pixel lay down on the couch in the sitting room. He didn't look well either. I sniffed his breath. He had been sneaking drinks at the Orange Peel. He would not be a happy orange cat in the morning. Abigail plopped down next to him and passed out. I paced back and forth. Charlotte was my problem now. She was a Tangledwood yet didn't seem to have any of their bloodline, not even a shade of Mrs. Tangledwood's aura. Something was quite different about her. She seemed in all likelihood to be human, but I had a cat sense about her. I leaped onto the window seat and stared onto the cobblestone street. I yawned and half closed my eyes. This was a problem that would wait till the morning.

I'm dreaming again. I hear high-pitched giggles. Prudence is lying next to me on the grass, staring up at the stars. My other sisters are doing the same each talking about their witch star. I look at Prudence as I did when I was a girl with love and acceptance even knowing what the future would bring.

"Terra, I'm going to visit my star as Elizabeth has. And when I do I'll come back as powerful as her."

"Prudence, it's late, and I worry we'll be found," I said.

"There's only a few minutes before May Day is finished. Let's enjoy them." She put her hand in mine. "Let's swear an oath on our witch stars, this night we swear we will always be sisters and best friends."

"I swear, Prudence."

"I swear, Terra—"

"What are you girls doing?"

I turned to see Farmer Johnson holding his lantern and a pitchfork. He lifted the lantern, trying to see our faces. We all scattered except Prudence, who stood slowly and walked toward him. "No Prudence," I screamed. It was too late.

She raised her hands, and his lantern extinguished. He gasped and pointed his pitchfork at her. She waved her hand as though swatting away a fly, and the pitchfork flew out of his hand. Prudence's eyes burned fire red. She began murmuring an incantation. I ran up to her and begged her, tears streaming down my face. She flung me away. "He knows us, Terra. The secret."

What happened next, I blocked from my memory or Elizabeth did. I'll never know for sure. The moment Master Johnson disappeared, Elizabeth appeared. She grabbed Prudence by the back of her hair. Prudence fell to the ground. "Forgive me, Elizabeth. I was protecting the coven."

"The oath, Prudence, you swore, the oath you promised never to harm a human. To use our powers for only good."

I felt a warm, wet sensation on the back of my head. I woke to see Pixel staring over me. "Me sorry, Terra. My tummy no good."

MR. TANGLEDWOOD'S WILD RIDE

ABIGAIL MOANED AND ROLLED OVER on the couch. I had pulled the afghan over her to ward off the evening chill. Pixel was still asleep on her feet.

Mrs. Twiggs came bounding down the stairs, humming. It was five thirty a.m. "Time to make the scones," she murmured. Thursday was scone day, Friday muffins, Saturday cinnamon buns, Sunday and Monday closed, Tuesday fluffy croissants buttery maybe some chocolate, some almond, Wednesdays donuts, but always fresh-baked iced cookies, petit fours and coffeecakes. Full breakfast usually consisted of egg soufflés, eggs courtesy of Henrietta and the girls from the small henhouse in the garden behind the Leaf & Page. Each day you could set a calendar by the smell coming out of the kitchen. Mrs. Twiggs stopped as she walked past the opening to the sitting room, walked backward and peeked in. "Terra, why's Abigail on the couch?"

"Mrs. Twiggs, I think we should have a talk."

She reached around the door, slipped her apron over her head, and tied it. She glanced at the cuckoo clock. "Okay, Terra, it has to be quick. The day is ticking away from us."

Albert gave her a wink from his portrait.

We sat at the small kitchen table. "Abigail was drinking last night and I'm afraid had a little too much. She is not feeling well."

"Where was she drinking? How? She's underage."

I gave her a look that like really, you don't think a witch could manage to acquire alcohol.

"I guess she's still a young girl trying to find herself."

"That's not all, Mrs. Twiggs. Charlotte was with us. There was an incident. Abigail used her magic."

"And Charlotte saw?"

"Yes."

"Oh, my this is a pickle. What do we do? Where is Charlotte? Is she okay?"

"Yes, Bryson followed her. She made it home to the Tangled-wood Estate. He made sure she got in safely."

Pixel stuck up his head, let out a crude belch, and closed his eyes again.

"Well, surely Charlotte must be aware that her great-aunt had magical powers. In fact, shouldn't Charlotte carry the same bloodline?"

"Not necessarily. I don't see any signs that she has any Wiccan blood."

"Oh, that's a shame. I had hoped..."

Before she could answer, I spoke. "I had hoped the same that she was our ninth Wiccan. There's something else we need to talk about. It concerns Mrs. Lund. I wasn't sure at first, but the night we went to the Biltmore basement and found her dead, I felt a presence. A ghost. I felt it again when we were doing inventory."

"Terra, I feel the presence of ghosts all throughout the Biltmore Estate. I can't see them like you do at least not yet. I'm still a novice, but I get inklings of their presence. Goose bumps. Chills on the back of my neck. That's what caught my attention. I couldn't see this ghost. I went and spoke with a friend of mine, a ghost friend of mine. He told me that the ghost I was sensing was a soldier from the Civil War."

I considered revealing the Dark Corner to Mrs. Twiggs, but it wasn't time. "I believe he knows what happened to Mrs. Lund. I don't think he killed her. Most ghosts don't have the ability to move objects in this world."

Mrs. Twiggs glanced over her shoulder. Albert had come to listen. He had his hand on her shoulder. She smiled even though she couldn't feel it. Albert smiled back. "How do we contact him?"

"I'm still puzzling that out."

"Terra, why can I see Albert but not the other ghosts?"

"Because Albert wants you to see him."

She smiled, smoothed her apron. Mrs. Twiggs was a woman of routine. She bustled around the kitchen, making batter and then baking her scones.

After the breakfast crowd left, Mrs. Twiggs took a tea break. Abigail finished washing dishes and sat down to join us. She did not look well; her face was pale and her eyes bloodshot. She plopped down next to Mrs. Twiggs and rubbed her eyes. "Okay, let's get this over. Everyone is thinking it. I screwed up. I used magic in front of a human. I get it. I was wrong," Abigail said.

"You must have terrified Charlotte. I can only imagine," Mrs. Twiggs said.

"Well, I wasn't thinking straight. She was in danger, and I tried to help her. She's my friend." Abigail turned defensive. "I'm going to go talk to her."

"You think that's a good idea? Terra said she is afraid of you. It must have been quite a shock."

"What do we do?"

"I think it's time we told her the truth about Mrs. Tangledwood," I said. "She has a right to know her family bloodline."

Mrs. Twiggs walked over and flipped the sign on the door to CLOSED. "We should go now," she said. We all climbed into her Volvo. Tracker hopped in the backseat next to Pixel, who swatted him on the nose. Tracker growled and snapped back. We arrived at the Tangledwood Estate in time to see Charlotte packing her Honda Accord. I thought how strange with so many exotic autos in the garage she was leaving in the car she came in. She froze when she saw us. Abigail ran out of the car and toward her. Charlotte inched slowly toward her driver door.

"Wait, Charlotte, let me explain," she said.

"Look, Abigail, I thought at first I imagined last night. I had a lot to drink. When I sobered up this morning, I couldn't shake that image, and then I saw the blood on my shirt. That really happened, didn't it?"

Mrs. Twiggs came over and put her arm around Charlotte. She had a calming effect in situations that arose such as this. "Charlotte, dear, Abigail is a good witch."

"Like of the North?" Charlotte asked with a half smile still taking a step back.

"Actually, dear, direction does play a very important role in the fairy world. Your great-aunt was a good Wiccan," Mrs. Twiggs said. "In fact she—"

"Wiccan?" Charlotte interrupted.

"Yes, dear, Wiccan—half mortal, half witch. A Wiccan comes from the bloodline of witches, but throughout years of mingling with humans, that bloodline thins. Some revert back to humans, other become Wiccans. Your great-aunt kept your bloodline and was a Wiccan."

"Does that mean you think I'm a Wiccan?"

Mrs. Twiggs smiled. "Not necessarily. I haven't seen any signs that you carry your aunt's bloodline."

"This is too much to take in. I didn't know my great-aunt. I'm here about my inheritance. This is too much for me." She paused. "I suppose you're a Wiccan too."

"Yes, dear, all the ladies of the Biltmore Society are Wiccans. We have been charged with keeping Asheville safe."

"Safe from what?"

"Just as there is good white magic, there's black magic that preys on the innocents."

"That's very interesting. I have to go now." Charlotte reached for her door handle.

As she did, I could smell the pipe smoke again coming from the garage. Abigail turned her head toward the garage. She smelled it too. She twitched her nose. We heard a car start. The garage door flew open, and the 1961 Mercedes convertible roared out of the garage and stopped inches in front of us, engine revving. Charlotte shook. "I don't like this. Is this black or white magic?"

Abigail stepped over to the car, putting a hand on the hood above the idling engine, and spoke an incantation. Mr. Tangled-wood showed himself to us. He was sitting in the driver's seat, wearing a driver's jacket, leather gloves and ascot, and smoking his pipe. He raised his hands in front of him, studying them as though he had never seen them before. He then looked at us, surprised and curious.

Charlotte said, "Who's that?"

"That's your great-uncle."

"My deceased great-uncle?" Charlotte reached for the door handle of her car.

Mr. Tangledwood tried to speak, but no words came out. Abigail placed her finger on his mouth and then he spoke. "Where am I? Who are you?"

"You are with the living. We are friends of your wife," Abigail said.

"You know Emma?"

"You know me, Beatrice." Mrs. Twiggs stepped closer to the car.

"Yes, Beatrice, I remember now. Emma speaks of you often."

"You've seen Emma recently?"

Mr. Tangledwood appeared confused. "Emma worries. She worries about her great-niece. She's been trying to reach out to her." Mr. Tangledwood vaporized; the car sped down the driveway and out of view. I could see Charlotte's head was spinning. This was too much for a girl her age, too much for any human.

"Abigail," I said. "Tell Charlotte that we'll—you'll—keep her safe."

"Char, believe me. I went through everything you're going through when I first got to Asheville. I was singing on the street, trying to make gas money. When I learned I was a witch, I thought I had finally gone crazy. I had heard voices in my head since I was a little girl. It wasn't a far stretch to think I'd finally lost it."

Charlotte slid down the car and sat on the pavement. She put her hands around her knees and slowly rocked. "This too much, too much."

Abigail sat next to her. "Look, last night I was trying to save you."

"Yes, I know. Thank you. If you hadn't come in, he would have, well you know."

"Yes, Char, I care about you. You're my friend. It's going to be all right. Really." Abigail put her arm around Charlotte's shoulders.

Charlotte looked up. "It's kind of cool having a best friend that's a witch. Think of all the trouble we can get into."

Abigail laughed. "That's it. That's the spirit."
"Don't say spirit please."
They both laughed.

CHARLOTTE'S TURNING

NOT OF MY CHOOSING BUT of circumstance, our coven had a human. Charlotte, though a relative of Emma Tangledwood, was not meant to close our circle of nine. She had learned the secret, and unlike my Salem coven, we were safe for now, but all the ladies of the coven needed to be assured that Charlotte would not lead them to any harm. Mrs. Twiggs drove us along the backwoods to the cabin. Abigail and Charlotte talked the entire way as though it was completely normal to be traveling to an enchanted cabin to meet with a coven of magical Wiccans.

When we arrived, Mrs. Branchworthy was waiting on the front porch in one of the rocking chairs. She rose to greet us. "The others will be here soon. Terra, I think I've—" Upon catching a glimpse of Charlotte, she stopped.

"Charlotte knows our secret. She's a friend," Abigail said.

Charlotte smiled. "Abigail told me that your specialty power is conjuring fire."

"Yes, dear."

"Can I see?"

Mrs. Branchworthy looked at Mrs. Twiggs, who nodded. Mrs. Branchworthy stepped off the porch. She placed her right hand palm up toward the sky and skimmed the top of it with the left. Fireballs shot into the sky like she was holding a roman candle.

"Awesome," Charlotte exclaimed. She turned to Mrs. Twiggs. "What can you do?"

Mrs. Twiggs said, "That's neither here nor there." Mrs. Twiggs was reluctant to let Charlotte in even though she was Emma's family. I shared her concern. Mrs. Twiggs was the unspoken leader of the coven. She felt that weight on her shoulders. The ladies arrived, and we all gathered inside the cabin as dusk was settling over the mountain. Abigail started the fire. Mrs. Twiggs brought in the tea service. All the ladies murmured asking why the meeting had been called and wanting to know why Charlotte was present.

Mrs. Twiggs tapped her teacup with her spoon. "Please, ladies, settle down. I will get right to the point. Charlotte knows what we are."

The murmurs began again. "Now, ladies, she's family. We can trust her."

Abigail moved her chair closer to Charlotte and held her hand. I leaped onto the table and spoke with Mrs. Twiggs.

Charlotte interrupted. "What's going on with the cat?"

Abigail said, "I've got some more news for you. Terra is a witch."

"You mean she turned herself into a cat." Charlotte reached for me, and I backed away.

"Actually, she was turned into a cat by my great-grandmother to protect her from the Salem witch trials. She's been stuck in that body since then."

Charlotte sat back in her chair. "Does she have a tiny cat flying broom and witch hat?" She smirked.

Abigail said, "Char, I know. When Terra first spoke to me."

"She can speak?" Charlotte interrupted.

"Of course she can. She's a witch."

"Why can't I understand her?"

"Because you're not."

"Let me get this straight. You're a witch, the cat's a witch, and they're all Wiccans." She pointed at the ladies. "What about the orange cat? Is he a hobbit or something?"

Abigail laughed. "No, Pixel's an ordinary cat. I'm sure it's a little confusing. Think of us all as magical superbeings."

"Like the League of Justice?"

"That's a good way to think of it. Anyway, Terra told me my life would never be the same. Once you awaken and see the magic in the world, you'll never look at the world the same way again. It's all around you, Char."

Charlotte sat quiet, trying to absorb everything Abigail was telling her. Pixel swiped a cookie off the serving tray. I was glad to see he was feeling better. The cookie landed on the floor, and Tracker made quick work of it. "Bad Tracker," Pixel scolded heading out the door in a huff.

Mrs. Twiggs said, "We've been tasked to watch over Charlotte. Mr. Tangledwood appeared to us at the Tangledwood Estate. Emma is worried about her great-niece."

Mrs. Stickman stood up. "Did you see Emma? Did you speak with her?"

Mrs. Twiggs shook her head. "Mr. Tangledwood only."

I highly doubted we would ever meet up again with Mrs. Tangledwood. She was taken from us by black magic. Mr. Tangledwood clung to her memory, which was soaked into the walls of their estate. His ghost was bound to the Mercedes convertible that had brought the two of them so much joy.

Charlotte raised her hand. "Can I say something?" All eyes turned toward her. "When I was a little girl, my favorite movie was *Bedknobs and Broomsticks*. So I'm good with this whole witch, Wiccan, talking cat thing." She paused. "Can you guys fly? Can I try a broomstick?"

"That's not how it works, but maybe you can," Abigail said. "You have your great-aunt's blood, so you *could* be a Wiccan."

"That's right. You can drink the potion," Mrs. Stickman said.

Charlotte stuttered. "No, I don't want to do that."

"Don't be afraid. It doesn't hurt, Char."

"No, really, I don't." Charlotte stood and walked toward the door.

Mrs. Raintree spoke. "Give her the potion, Beatrice. It worked for all of us."

Mrs. Twiggs said, "We can try."

Unlike the other ladies before they turned, I did not see any spark of Wiccan in Charlotte, but it was worth trying. It would satisfy our curiosity. Mrs. Twiggs hurried into the kitchen and prepared the turning potion.

Abigail went outside with me on her heels. "There you are."

Charlotte sat on the step, smoking a cigarette.

Abigail sat next to her. "Really, there's nothing to be afraid of, and it will put the ladies' minds at ease. We've been looking for our ninth Wiccan to close the coven."

Charlotte threw her cigarette to the ground, smashing it out with her foot. "They are not going to leave it alone until you drink the potion," Abigail said.

"Okay." She stood up, and they went back in the house. As we entered, Charlotte whispered," Is this safe? Does it taste bad?"

"All the ladies drank it, and they're fine."

Mrs. Twiggs handed Charlotte a teacup.

"Okay." Charlotte downed it like it was a shot of whiskey. Her eyes darted around the room, waiting for something to happen. All the ladies held their breath, waiting for her to rise off the ground, her hair to turn raven black and the telltale white streak. But nothing. "How long does this take?" Charlotte asked.

Mrs. Twiggs came close, felt Charlotte's forehead with the back of her hand, and looked closely into her eyes. "It should have happened by now."

Charlotte looked relieved as all the ladies let out their breath and sat back down. Charlotte walked out onto the porch, and Abigail followed. I jumped onto the railing and sat quietly, listening.

"Yeah, I know. It's a lot, but it's a lot of responsibility too. You saw what happened to me at the bar."

"Abigail, all my life I've felt like an outsider. My parents never paid attention to me. Don't get me wrong. They weren't bad people. They had their own problems."

"You fit in here, Char, and I'm your friend." Abigail paused. "I'm an outsider too. The ladies are a coven of Wiccans, and I'm a witch. Your aunt was the ninth Wiccan, which completed the coven. They are broken without her, but you are part of our family—magic or not."

"Tell me, Abigail. Tell me the truth. What happened to her?"

Abigail went into the cabin and brought out her family spell book. She placed it on her lap. "This book is thousands of years old. It was my great-grandmother's, Elizabeth. The head of Terra's coven in Salem. It's a very powerful book of spells that only my bloodline, the Oakhaven, can wield. One of Terra's sisters in her coven, Prudence, stole the book. The book is neither black nor white magic. Prudence wanted the book for selfish reasons. That opened a portal to black magic through the book. The book called out to her and possessed her. Your great-aunt found the book. It possessed her too. In the end it destroyed her."

"And now you have the book, Abigail? What does that make you?"

"I'd only use the book for good as my foremothers have but Terra won't let me open it yet. She thinks I'm not ready."

"Aren't you dying to look inside?"

Abigail nodded.

"What's stopping you?"

I jumped on top of the book and hissed. "Abigail, put the book away." My fur stood up; my tail puffed out. I was not happy with this new Abigail. She was careless. I looked over at Charlotte.

"Nice kitty," she said, running her hand down my back. I hissed and took off in search of Pixel. Abigail wasn't the only one I was worried about. Pixel had not been himself lately. I leaped the stones in the stream, trying to keep dry, and followed the path to the valley. No sign of Pixel. It was getting late, way past his supper-time. I followed the stream through the valley to the little gulley garden where I had seen Pixel playing the other day. I stopped when I heard the scream.

"Pixel," I yelled and ran as fast as I could, following the sound of Pixel's agony.

When I reached the gulley, I saw a large crow swooping and pecking at Pixel. It wasn't just a large crow, it was the largest crow I had ever seen. Its figure was distorted and elongated. In its beak it clasped the purple-and-white butterfly that had landed on Pixel's nose. Pixel leaped in the air higher than I thought a fluffy orange cat with crooked little legs could. He grabbed the crow by its wing and pulled it to the ground, forcing it to release the butterfly. Then he stood up on his hind paws and extended all his front claws. The crow took off before Pixel could wreak his vengeance.

"Pixel, are you okay?"

He turned to me with blood all over his fur—some his, some the crow's. "Bad bird, Terra. Bad bird. Take my friend."

I threw my paws around him. The thought of losing Pixel terrified me. Not just because I loved this silly alley cat but because Pixel was my best friend. He was unconditional with his love and his courage. He was also my familiar. He had once told me he liked to be my familiar, and I thought how funny that a witch that was a cat would have a cat familiar. Now I couldn't imagine it any other way. The purple-and-white butterfly floated down. She was no worse for the wear. Somehow I knew it was a she. Her delicate wings, the way she landed softly on Pixel's back. She fluttered once and twice and then took off into the mountain ash. My witch tree, I thought.

"Terra."

"Yes, Pixel."

"Pixel miss supper?" he asked as we hurried our pace through the valley.

"No, Pixel."

I stepped carefully into the woods. Too many lights danced in the woods at night. Some smelled of pure happiness, others smelled of death. It made me nervous.

Whereas I with much less courage was afraid to be in these woods after dark, Pixel feared the fate of missing supper. I watched him from the corner of my eye as we ran and jumped through the woods. He, too, kept an eye to our flank. Pixel was protecting me from the night creatures that watched from the shadows. We reached the cabin in time to find Mrs. Twiggs serving up the beef stew.

"Me favorite." Pixel rushed to the table, pushing Tracker and me out of the way.

All the ladies gathered around the table, smiling and making light conversation. "Pixel, wait your turn," I told him. I looked around the table at the smiling faces that had no idea of what was coming, and I would leave it that way.

Mrs. Twiggs placed bowls of food for Pixel and me. Tracker was not allowed on the table, but it didn't stop him from snapping at Pixel. Pixel swatted him on the nose as he leaped onto the table. Pixel finished before me.

"Terra. We keep Flutter safe," he said.

I looked up. "Who?"

"Pixel friend, Flutter. Butterfly."

"Yes, of course, Pixel, we'll do whatever we can to protect her."

"Good, Terra." He gazed up at Mrs. Twiggs with Margaret Keane eyes begging for more.

The ladies left early per my request. I did not want them traveling after dark. Mrs. Loblolly stayed behind because Mrs. Twiggs insisted they speak. Mrs. Raintree sat by the fire, finishing a dream catcher she was making for Charlotte.

Strumming her guitar, Abigail sat with Charlotte on the porch. Charlotte stared at her phone. One of Abigail's first incantations was a modified version of a spell to conjure voices over great distance to communicate with friends in times of danger. Prudence and I had used that incantation to talk at night between our houses. Abigail found a way to turn that into the internet in the middle of the Black Mountain woods without a cell tower within range. Charlotte had never questioned how she was able to use the Wi-Fi on her phone.

"June, I asked you to stay because we need to talk about Mrs. Lund," Mrs. Twiggs said.

"Beatrice, I told you everything I knew. She contacted me about the colonel and told me she had additional information about him and his regiment." Mrs. Loblolly paused. "I feel horrible. I told you I feel responsible. She came here because of me and died by my great-grandfather's sword."

Mrs. Twiggs put her arm around Mrs. Loblolly. "It's not your fault. She lied to you. She misrepresented who she was."

"But I donated the sword. I demanded that they pose the mannequin to appear as if he was charging into battle. How selfish of me. How careless. That sword was as sharp as the day the colonel rode into battle. I had it cleaned and polished for the display. I even had to bring it to a special swordsmith because the blade is pure silver. It was his dress sword."

"What?" I interrupted. "The blade was silver? Not just the hilt?"

"Yes, the colonel appreciated things of quality. His uniforms were custom made and fitted, the buttons are gold, and he ordered that sword special from a swordsmith in England."

"What's wrong, Terra?" Mrs. Twiggs asked.

"Silver through the heart is a true death to a witch."

"Terra, are you saying Mrs. Lund was a witch?"

"There's only one way to find out for sure. We have to see the body. If she was a witch and she died by silver, her body will age to its witch years. If I was killed by silver, all you'd see is bones and dust. We have to leave now before dark."

"The mannequin holding the colonel's sword was wearing a lieutenant's uniform, not a colonel's. If you spent so much money on restoring the sword, why not stage it with the colonel's uniform?"

"That can't be right. I donated the colonel's uniform and was insistent that it be displayed with his sword."

Pixel trotted by, his snowy belly flopping right and left along the floor of the cabin. He jumped into the windowsill as the sun was setting. He turned to us and solemnly said, "By the pricking of my thumb, something wicked this way comes."

I leaped onto the windowsill next to him, staring into the distance. I felt it too. "Pixel, are you okay?" I whispered, nuzzling up to him.

"Me scared, Terra." He put his paw around my neck and snuggled closer to me. I found his warmth comforting, his heartbeat next to mine soothing.

I thought about the stirrings in the wood. "Mrs. Twiggs, it's late. I think we should rest tonight. Mrs. Lund isn't going anywhere," I said.

THE VINE THAT
KILLED THE SOUTH

W E DARTED OUTSIDE AS WE heard the screams from the porch. Charlotte and Abigail were being dragged down the steps, their legs tied by a creeping green vine, pulling them toward the woods. The vine continued wrapping them into a cocoon until their screams were muffled. I heard Abigail gasping, trying to say incantations. Pixel and I jumped on the vine, gnawing and clawing at it. "Terra, nothing's working," Abigail said through strained breaths as the vine tightened around her.

Mrs. Twiggs flew down the stairs, brandishing a kitchen knife. She cut at the vines, but as quickly as she did, they grew back.

"Kudzu," Mrs. Raintree yelled. "It's the vine that killed the south. You can't cut it. It grows back faster and stronger."

It wrapped around Mrs. Twiggs's legs. She cut at it feverishly, scraping her legs with the knife. Mrs. Loblolly and Mrs. Raintree pulled at the vines, trying to free Mrs. Twiggs. Mrs. Loblolly fell to the ground, and the vine wrapped around her throat. She tugged at it, gasping for air. Tracker barked and jumped around the vines, trying not to be entangled. His sharp bark pierced the still night. Abigail and Charlotte disappeared into the woods. I leaped from vine to vine until it wrapped around my paw and pulled me to the ground.

Pixel screamed. "No, Terra, no."

"Pixel, run," I yelled. "Save yourself."

"No, Terra." He jumped on the vine that wrapped around my legs, clawing and snapping at it. The vine reached for him, pulling me into the woods farther away from the cabin. Pixel stepped back, staring.

Through the tight green vine, I saw Mrs. Raintree jump on the cabin railing as the kudzu wrapped its way around the post, searching hungrily for her flesh. Pixel turned and ran up to the porch. He crawled up her leg until she picked him up and held him. "You fix."

"What Pixel?"

"You fix now."

She understood. The last thing I heard was Mrs. Raintree singing a Cherokee war dance song, the same one I had heard Agatha Hollows sing. The vine wrapped around my eyes, blinding me. I felt the air leaving me as my lungs collapsed. Elizabeth came to me. She was glowing white with silvery angel wings, her skin ethereal. She sat on the edge of Poinsett Bridge. She didn't speak, motioning for me to come to her with open arms so she could embrace me. I gasped as my lungs filled with air again. The kudzu shriveled and fell off me. It took me a minute to capture my breath as I looked around. I was deep in the woods past the stream. I ran back to the cabin. Charlotte and Abigail were hugging Mrs. Twiggs. Pixel ran and tackled me. He licked my face and picked pieces of the dead vine off me. "Terra clean now," he said.

Wanda Raintree is a steward of the earth like her goddess foremother, Elinhino. She has the power to nourish the soil, to feed the plants and the trees. Somehow Pixel knew she also had the ability to extract those nutrients, starving the kudzu to death. "Thank you, my friend. You saved us all, Pixel. How did you know she could do that?" I asked him.

"Me friend told me," he said, running back into the cabin. I glanced around at the enchanted woods. How could the kudzu enter this sacred space? Only twice had the enchantment been broken. The last time was when the lieutenant came for Agatha Hollows.

Mrs. Twiggs bent down and picked me up. She looked at me. There was no terror in her eyes. I could hear her heartbeat slow and steady. She was at peace. "Terra, I think we should go see about Mrs. Lund now." I agreed.

RIP, MRS. LUND

MRS. TWIGGS SPED ALONG THE dirt road, descending Black Mountain. I sat in the passenger seat, my eyes darting back and forth. The trees crackled and closed behind our path, guarding the road to the cabin. I knew all would be safe there tonight. Mrs. Raintree blessed the trees that barred the way to the cabin. She had absorbed the magic left by Agatha Hollows. That magic combined with her bloodline from her Cherokee goddess mother increased her powers tenfold.

We reached the Asheville city morgue where Mrs. Lund was being held pending the autopsy and police investigation. I hoped the autopsy had not been performed yet, because if it had and she was a witch, they would have found that she was a two or three or maybe five-hundred-year-old skeleton.

Mrs. Twiggs politely knocked on the door. A young man wearing earbuds and a county morgue button-down shirt answered. "Yes, ma'am. What can I do for you?" he asked, removing one bud from one ear.

She smiled and blew a little dust from the palm of her hand over him. He returned her smile and let us in. Then he walked back to his office chair, put his legs up on the desk, and picked up a graphic novel. We found our way to the holding room with a wall of cold chambers. Mrs. Twiggs and I gave our respects to the dearly departed who stood around the room. We said a little prayer. "Terra, can't we help these poor souls?" Mrs. Twiggs asked.

"They don't know that they've passed yet. They're still attached to their earthly vessel."

Mrs. Twiggs raised her hands. "Gentle souls release yourselves from this earthly plain. Join your loved ones as I speak your name." Mrs. Twiggs walked in front of each cold chamber, each one labeled with a name. As she called off each name, they thanked her and disappeared. Finally we came to Mrs. Lund's chamber.

"Are you ready for this, Mrs. Twiggs?" I asked.

"Yes, Terra dear." When she pulled the drawer open, it was worse than I thought. There was nothing. The chamber was empty. "Where's the body, Terra?"

Mrs. Twiggs went up to the security guard. He pulled his ear-buds out, his eyes still twinkling from the enchantment. "Dear, you're missing a body. Mrs. Lund. Contact Detective Willows, and we were never here," Mrs. Twiggs said.

"You were never here," he repeated, smiling before reaching for the phone.

Mrs. Twiggs waved her hand over the surveillance monitors, erasing any record of us entering the building or leaving it.

WHAT ABOUT ALBERT?

"SHE'S GONE, TERRA," MRS. TWIGGS said with a bemused air.

"She can't be a witch, Mrs. Twiggs, or a human."

"Terra, that leaves a lot of choices in between doesn't it, dear? I felt what you have, the awakenings in the wood and even in downtown Asheville. The good and the evil. We've thrown a pebble into the pond of magic, and the ripple has gone out. How do we find her, Terra?" Mrs. Twiggs reached in her cloak pocket and felt the leather pouch that Mrs. Owen had given her. "Terra, we have to try the premonition potion again. We have to know what's coming our way, and we have to find Mrs. Lund."

We hurried to the Leaf & Page, which was ablaze with light. "That's funny. I don't remember leaving the lights on." Mrs. Twiggs fiddled with her key at the door. She unlocked it and called out for Albert. She screamed in horror when she saw his picture shattered on the floor. "Albert," she screamed again with no response.

Then we glanced around the room to find it in complete disarray. Books were thrown off shelves, tables overturned. The only clue left behind was the smell of electricity, a burning copper taste in my mouth, a singed smell in my nostrils. The smell that a ghost leaves in its wake but not a friendly ghost. "How can this be, Terra? I enchanted the store. Albert kept watch. Where is he? Where's Albert?" Mrs. Twiggs strained to hold back her tears.

"They took him, Mrs. Twiggs. The ghosts took him."

"Why? Terra, he can't defend himself. He doesn't know he's a ghost."

"Mrs. Twiggs, take me to the Fillmore." I hoped that Bradley might have some answers.

We rushed out the door and headed to the Fillmore. Bradley greeted us, never moving from attention as the guests, some alive some less than alive, walked into the hotel. "Little miss," he said with a smile. "You're back. And you brought a friend."

"This is Mrs. Twiggs. Her husband, Albert Twiggs is missing," I said.

"Yes, of course." He nodded politely as a guest went by. "I've had occasion to exchange hellos with Mr. Twiggs. A fine gentleman, speaks the world of you, Mrs. Twiggs."

"Have you seen him tonight?"

"No, little miss. I have not, then again I've been so busy with all the new arrivals," Bradley said.

I looked around, hoping to see Albert. I saw ghosts both new and old, more than I've ever seen, not just entering the Fillmore but strolling the streets around Pack Square. Some garbed in today's wear, others in gilded-age finery. Across the street by the fountain I saw one such apparition in his evening coat, opening and closing his pocket watch. The rocking chair man, his soulless dark orbs staring through me from across the street. Mrs. Twiggs couldn't see him. The ghosts couldn't see him. Only I, a witch, could see him. He was a familiar from another world. Mrs. Owen had traveled to another world and brought him back. He snapped his watch shut after counting thirteen times. He smiled a toothless grin. Then he climbed up the side of the Jackson Building, crawling like a maleficent spider on all four appendages, a shadow darting along a serpentine web, and then he was gone.

"Terra, what are you looking at?"

"All the ghosts. I thought I saw someone I knew."

"Little miss, I almost had forgotten that soldier boy was back. I told him he might try the Leaf & Page to find you. I told him it was one of your favorite haunts," Bradley said with a smile and wink.

"Thank you, Bradley. Please let me know if you hear from Albert or the soldiers," I told him.

"Of course, little miss."

We turned and went back to the car. "It's too late to go back to the cabin."

"Terra, I have to be at the store for opening." Mrs. Twiggs's way of dealing with tragedy was to stick to her routine. I respected that.

"Mrs. Twiggs, are you okay? Are you okay to go back there?"

"Yes, I hope whoever took Albert does come back," she said with a steadfast look. I almost felt pity for the criminal who would have to deal with the wrath of Beatrice Twiggs.

We spent the rest of the night cleaning up the mess at the Leaf & Page, Mrs. Twiggs doing most of the work. I did what I could. My first priority was making the store safe from intruders. I should have known better than to leave it unprotected with all the activity around Asheville. I underestimated the power of the black magic that was rising. Albert was no match for his captors, and they had broken right through Mrs. Twiggs's enchantment spells. The only person that could have stopped them was Abigail, and she was in no state of mind to battle the apparitions that had taken over. She was not ready. She was still a girl. I walked along the top of the bookshelf, eying each spine until I reached the book I sought. It was a book on Appalachian folklore. The pages were worn and tattered, but they held the answers we so desperately needed. The mountainfolk had fought dark spirits for hundreds of years in the Carolinas. By trial and error they came across spells and potions that only the most advanced witches would know. Agatha Hollows knew the people living in these mountains understood the power of the woods. I grabbed the spine of the book with my teeth, pulling at it until it fell to the floor. Mrs. Twiggs turned around. "This is what we need, Mrs. Twiggs," I said.

She picked up the book and sat by the fire. "With all the spell books and witches' potions we have, you want us to rely on human folklore?"

"Folklore is based in truth. The spirits we are fighting come from these woods. The creature that took the form of Mrs. Lund and the ghost that took Albert they're from these woods. They have been dormant until we woke them with our white magic. They are as much a part of these mountains and woods as you and the coven are."

"Very well, Terra." Mrs. Twiggs ran through the receipts, as the Appalachian folk called them. Following their advice, she gathered sage and burned it in each corner of the room. She laid salt at all the windows and doorsteps. When she had finished, she placed the frame that held Albert's image and his ghost over the cash register. It was five thirty a.m. Friday, which meant muffins. Mrs. Twiggs let in the others, the stray cats and dogs from the alley. When they were done feeding, she opened the store for the humans. It was a slow day—some usual customers, a few out-of-towners looking for first editions and specialty teas. As we were about to close, Detective Willows pulled up and squeezed himself out of his unmarked police car. By his solemn look, I thought he was not here for pleasantries.

"Oh, Detective, I was just closing," Mrs. Twiggs said as he came in the front door.

"Beatrice, I'm here on official business. We need to talk. Can we sit for a bit?" Detective Willows said, his face distressed.

"Of course."

He sat at one of the small café tables in the dining room.

"Can I get you anything? I think I have some muffins left or scones."

"No thank you." He pulled out his notebook. "I have to ask where you were last night around ten p.m."

Beatrice Twiggs cannot tell a lie. It is not in her. Even at the risk of incriminating herself, she stared at Detective Willows. "What is this about, Butch?"

"There was an incident at the county morgue last night. We checked the traffic camera on the street, and your car was parked out in front of the morgue. Were you driving it?"

"Yes, I was, Butch."

"Why were you at the morgue last night?"

"I went to see Mrs. Lund's body."

"Why did you do that?"

I held my breath waiting to hear Mrs. Twiggs' response.

"Because she was killed with a silver sword. I thought she might be a witch," Mrs. Twiggs said.

Detective Willows burst out laughing. "Oh, Beatrice, you are a card."

"Butch, look around you. I've spent the past ten years collecting vintage books, tales of the occult, spell books. I have healing stones, special herbs, and love potions. When June Loblolly told me the colonel's sword was pure silver, I thought that whoever killed Mrs. Lund believed she was a witch and that was the only way to end her existence."

"Beatrice, I don't believe the witch part, but I do believe she was murdered. I don't think a mannequin would just accidentally fall over and land on top of her, stabbing a sword through her heart. However, without a body, I can't prove murder."

"What are you saying?" Mrs. Twiggs asked, hiding her knowledge of the missing Mrs. Lund.

"I'm saying Mrs. Lund's body is missing from the morgue. The security guard has no record of anyone entering the building. I checked the surveillance tapes, and nobody came in or out last night. And I checked back several days, and Mrs. Lund certainly did not walk out of the building. I had to ask you why you were in the area." He paused for a moment. "Beatrice, it's more than Mrs. Lund. There been a lot of unusual activity."

"What do you mean, Butch?"

"At the cemetery by the River Arts District, headstones have been knocked over and graves dug up," Butch said. This was new to me. I hadn't known any of this was happening. He continued, "I wrote it off as kids getting into mischief but then the 911 calls started coming in reporting floating orbs in the woods, flickering lights, and whispers at city hall."

"Is there something you're not telling me, Butch?"

"Beatrice, I wouldn't say this to anyone else but you. But I could have sworn I saw Annabelle. It was a flash of her out of the corner of my eye. I was walking down Biltmore Avenue in broad daylight, and I swore I saw her walking in the crowd."

"Butch, that's not so unusual. You miss her and think about her." Mrs. Twiggs reached over and took his hand.

"No, it's more than that. It was her. She didn't turn around, but

I know that profile. I know the back of her head. I know the way she walks. It was her, Beatrice. I haven't told anyone else because they would think I was crazy or senile, but I knew you would understand with all the books you've read on the paranormal."

Mrs. Twiggs released his hand and sat back. "Butch, there's a lot more unnatural in this world than the natural. I believe our spirit moves on but also leaves traces of who we were. It's possible that your wife wasn't ready to move on. She misses you and is looking for you."

Butch stared at the empty frame over the cash register. "Where's your picture of Albert?"

"It fell and broke."

"Do you ever have the feeling like he's watching over you?"

"Yes, all the time."

"That's all I came to say." He slid the chair back from the table and stood.

"Hold on just a minute." She walked over to the counter that was filled with healing stones. She handed him a milky light green stone. "This is apophyllite. It will connect you with spirits." She then handed him a clear stone. "This is clear quartz. It is the ultimate amplifier. It boosts the energy of any crystal you use. When you see Annabelle, even a glimpse of her, hold up the quartz. You'll be able to look at her directly through the stone. She'll be drawn to it. It will help lift the veil between you two."

"I'm not buying into this." He shook his head and then grabbed the stones, putting them in his pocket.

Mrs. Twiggs interrupted. "You miss her deeply. I know, Butch. Keep the stones in your pocket. No one has to know."

He gave her a half smile. As he walked out, he reached over and petted my head. His plump big fingers nearly knocked me over, but I could tell he was a kind soul. Still I pulled away. I leaped up on the end table and said, "Mrs. Twiggs."

"I know, Terra. How do we stop the black magic that's awakening? What creatures are coming? What creatures are real? I've read every book on the supernatural and on monsters and myth. What is true, Terra?"

"There's a little bit of truth in all those books. The monsters are the ones we create from our dark sides. They feed off our jealousies, our anger. They feed off those emotions. We put that negative energy out into the universe, and then it comes back to destroy us, but just as that negative energy comes back so does the good energy. We have to find our army, Mrs. Twiggs. The battle is coming."

The silver bell above the door jingled. We both glanced toward the door to see Abigail and Charlotte come in. They were both wearing green army jackets. Abigail was carrying Pixel, Tracker by her side. "Mrs. Twiggs, check out what Char and I picked up at the thrift store. Pretty authentic, what do you think?" Abigail spun around, showing off her jacket.

FAHRENHEIT 451

IT WAS SUPPERTIME, AND MRS. Twiggs had once again made honey-baked ham, Pixel's favorite. He was on his second, no, third helping. Charlotte and Abigail chattered throughout dinner while Mrs. Twiggs sat in contemplation. I also pondered the recent events and maintained my own counsel.

"So, Mrs. Twiggs, Abigail told me about Albert. Is it true that he's a ghost?" Charlotte asked.

Mrs. Twiggs picked up the serving platter with the remaining ham. Without saying a word, she carried it into the kitchen.

"Terra, what's wrong?" Abigail asked.

"Albert's missing."

"What do you mean missing?"

"He was taken."

"Taken by whom, Terra?"

"By the same apparitions that tried to kill Mrs. Lund."

"What do you mean tried to kill? She had a saber plunged

through her heart," Abigail said.

"Mrs. Twiggs and I went to examine her body at the morgue, and it was gone."

"What happened to it?"

"Mrs. Lund was neither a witch nor a human."

"What does that leave, Terra?"

"That's what we're trying to find out tonight. Don't speak of Albert. Mrs. Twiggs is very worried about him as am I."

Abigail sat back in her chair. She put her iPhone down on the table. In a matter of a few minutes I saw her turn from a carefree teenager into the adult witch. The gravity of my words settled hard upon her. She had been avoiding the inevitable. She was the leader of us all; only she could protect us from what was coming. She had been running from that responsibility. "Terra, what can I do?"

"You can get back to studying your spell books and concentrate on sharpening your powers."

"Yes of course. What about Albert? What can we do for him?"

"Help Mrs. Twiggs make the premonition potion and be careful with the hogweed. I don't trust the dependability of Mrs. Owen's wares. They are more powerful than she lets on," I cautioned her.

"Yes of course."

"Abigail what's going on? It sounds serious," Charlotte said. It was then I realized that she had been listening to half the conversation. I had forgotten she couldn't understand me.

"Charlotte, maybe you should go stay at the estate," Abigail said.

"I'm not going back there."

"I can't keep you safe here." Sensing Abigail's frustration, Tracker came and lay down on her feet.

"You said you would protect me."

I looked at the beautiful Abigail just the age that Elizabeth was when she led our coven. Her shoulders drooped as did Elizabeth's as though the weight of the world was truly upon them. The price of leadership is the loss of innocence.

Abigail went into the kitchen to help Mrs. Twiggs make the potion. We adjourned to the sitting room by the fire. Mrs. Twiggs sat in Emma Tangledwood's chair. Abigail walked behind her and placed both her hands on Mrs. Twiggs's shoulders, who held the potion in her most expensive teacup, Meissen. It bubbled in the teacup. Mrs. Twiggs glanced down. A plume of green smoke rose from the teacup and momentarily took the form of the face of Karen Owen and then dissipated into the ceiling. Mrs. Twiggs drank the potion.

Pixel whispered, "Me no like" and then covered his eyes with his paws.

Tracker howled and then lay across Abigail's feet. Mrs. Twiggs's head slumped to her chest. She dropped the teacup. It shattered on the hardwood floor. The fire went out with a whoosh of cold air. Frost framed the windows. I could see my breath in front of me. My cat heart was beating twice as fast as a cat heart should. I smelled the electricity in the air. EMT. Electromagnetic. They were here watching. Mrs. Twiggs leaped from her chair. Her arms extended. Her eyes were milky white. Her hair blew back as though she were in a windstorm. She turned her head and stared directly at me. The voice that came out of her was not her own.

"You know the path you must take, Terra Rowan. The hunters are here. They've taken the ghost Albert. The creature that you call Mrs. Lund, she comes for the same purpose as they. You are the key, Terra Rowan. They will not stop until you lead them to it. No one is safe. Head south." Mrs. Twiggs collapsed to the floor.

Abigail ran to her side. The fire burst to uncontrollable flames licking at the mantle. Emma Tangledwood's chair caught on fire and then the reading lamp. Abigail tried to wake Mrs. Twiggs. In a matter of minutes, the entire sitting room was ablaze. Thick smoke filled our lungs. Charlotte and Abigail grabbed Mrs. Twiggs by the arms and dragged her into the dining room. They ran for a fire extinguisher, but before they could reach it, a fiery whip cracked and snatched it from the wall. The whip cracked again, knocking over shelves of old books that took to flames. The roar was deafening.

"Charlotte, we have to get everyone out," Abigail screamed.

Abigail raised her hand. Mrs. Twiggs floated off the floor. The girls ran out the front door with Pixel, Tracker, and me behind. Mrs. Twiggs floating all the way out. We all collapsed to the ground, coughing. In the distance we could hear the sirens coming close. Mrs. Twiggs came to. She saw her beloved Leaf & Page burning to the ground and tried to run back in. Abigail and Charlotte grabbed her, holding her back. Abigail tried every incantation she knew, but none could quench the thirst of the flames.

We watched all night as the Asheville Fire Department worked to control the blaze and protect the adjacent buildings. It was daybreak. All that was left was brick walls and smoldering timbers. Mrs. Twiggs's entire life had gone up in smoke in front of her. She sat on the bench across the street. She was wearing the blanket that the EMTs had wrapped around her after she refused any medical treatment. A handsome young fireman came up to her, carrying a clucking Henrietta under his arm.

"Thank you," Mrs. Twiggs said, holding out her arms for the chicken. I sat on her lap, trying to console her. "Terra, I saw them. I saw the ghosts that took Albert. They were wearing Confederate uniforms. There were two privates and a lieutenant. I couldn't make out their faces, but I could feel their hatred. I could feel their evil, Terra, except for one of the privates. He was scared, I believe, and sorry for what he was doing. They said they would spare our lives in exchange for you. They said they would give me back Albert if I gave them you. What do they want from you, Terra?"

"Those were the men that came for Agatha Hollows. They said they were coming to requisition supplies from area farms. Agatha told me they were witch hunters. They wanted to use her powers against their enemies. The lieutenant wasn't like the others. He had a different purpose."

"Terra, what are we going to do?"

"They want me to take them to the last place on earth that Agatha Hollows walked in her human form. I can't do that."

"Why not?"

"Because the magic that lays waiting there can destroy all of humankind. That's the lieutenant's purpose."

WITCH HUNTERS

B ISCUIT HEAD WAS ASHEVILLE'S BEST biscuits and breakfast servings, short of course of Mrs. Twiggs's muffins and
scones. The ladies of the Biltmore Society sat around the small café,
drinking tea and picking at dinner-plate-sized biscuits although
none had an appetite. They rallied around Mrs. Twiggs.

"Beatrice, you said that they were wearing Confederate uniforms. Did you notice any special markings?" Mrs. Loblolly asked.

"Yes, June, they all had the North Carolina home guard patch
on their sleeve."

"That was the colonel's regiment. After he was wounded, he ran
the entire Western North Carolina home guard. Those men would
have been under his command," Mrs. Loblolly said.

"They weren't looking for deserters or protecting the boarders,
June. They were witch hunters trying to turn the tide of the war
by harnessing Agatha Hollows's power. Think of all the innocent
humans who were abducted or killed by them believing they were

witches." Mrs. Twiggs swirled the cream in her coffee.

"But I've never read anything about the Confederates using supernatural powers to fight the Union," Mrs. Loblolly said.

"It's not something in the history books. It was a very secret task force."

"I can't believe my great-great-grandfather would have anything to do with hunting witches. The Loblollies have always had some touch of magic in our bloodline. My grandmother would tell me stories of clairvoyants, mediums. It wasn't until my turning that I realized I come from a long line of witches as you all. My great-great-grandfather must have had some inkling that he, too, came from a bloodline of magic."

"Maybe that's why they were hunting Agatha Hollows. They believed that magic was real and that's why he carried the silver-bladed saber. He knew from the folklore of the Appalachians that silver could kill a witch."

Mrs. Loblolly stood up and pounded the table. "That's enough. I won't have you talk about my family like that. I'm sorry, Beatrice you've been through so much. Forgive me but I will not hear that."

TAKE ME TO THE RIVER

I KNEW WHAT I HAD TO do. I knew from the moment Agatha Hollows disappeared under the bridge that I would have to return someday. The hunters had seen me. The young men—really boys—didn't see the real me, but the lieutenant knew who and what I was. He has hunted me ever since. I'd have to say goodbye to my friends. I crept into Mrs. Twiggs's room. She had taken over Mrs. Tangledwood's master bedroom. She was still asleep. I nuzzled her head. She woke with a smile.

"Terra, I can't let you go. I know what you're thinking. It's too dangerous. Not just for you but all of us. What will we do if we lose you?"

"You have Abigail; she is your leader."

"Abigail is still just a girl. She's not ready to take on that responsibility. She's afraid."

"Mrs. Twiggs, if I don't go you'll never see Albert again. There are worse things than death. None of you, especially Abigail, will be safe if I stay." I knew this day had been coming, but I'd been selfish in my search to find my Elizabeth. "I've shirked my responsibilities to you, my coven." I paused. "I was afraid."

Before Mrs. Twiggs could answer, I leaped off the bed. Abigail was in the next bedroom, rocking in the chair by the window, staring into the distant nothingness. A book lay open on her lap. It was *The Legend of Sleepy Hollow* by Washington Irving. Curious but appropriate reading. She snapped it closed and pointed it at me. "Terra, do you realize who?" She paused. "What you are about to confront?"

"Yes, Abigail." I knew what the creature was when it was covered in flesh. It carries its evil now in the spirit world. Agatha Hollows killed the flesh, but she couldn't kill the spirit. There's only one way to do that in this world. I believe Agatha left that to me. "The creature is a Dullahan, a headless horseman. It is the only creature that could break through the woods surrounding Agatha Hollows's cabin and the enchantment Mrs. Twiggs had placed on the Leaf & Page. The whip it carries is made from the corpse of a human spine. His wagon is covered in dried human skin. When the Dullahan stops riding, that is where a person is going to die. It calls out the person's name, and that is when that person perishes. He has come to call our names. There's no way to stop him as a spirit, Abigail, he must die when he is flesh."

"Terra, I can't let you go. It's too dangerous," Abigail said. "You can't leave me here alone. I can't do this without you. I have so much to learn."

I wanted to tell her that I would be back, but I knew it wasn't true. "Abigail, you're strong. You're the strongest witch I've ever known. Everything you need is inside you. Embrace your bloodline."

Abigail didn't turn to say goodbye. She couldn't.

There was one last room I had to enter. I stopped outside Pixel's room, trying to find words to say to him that would make him understand. He was asleep on the featherbed, upside down, his white belly sprawled out, paws kneading the air, giggling. "Flutter," he repeated. I leaped on the bed next to him and stared at him. What a wonderful creature this Pixel is. He flung his eyes open and leaped on me. We bounced in the fluffy down comforter playing like cats should. Then he stopped. "What wrong, Terra? Why

Terra sad?"

"Pixel, I have to leave for a while."

"Pixel go." He tumbled around the bed.

"Not this time. I need you to stay here and watch over Abigail and the ladies."

"Terra no go."

"It's important, Pixel. I'll be back soon. I promise."

All the joy flushed out of his face. I couldn't bear to look at him any longer. I scurried out of the room, down the spiral staircase, and out the kitchen doggie door. Tracker was waiting for me outside. I rubbed my head against his chin. "Guard Abigail with your life and be nice to Pixel, okay?"

He wiggled his tailless behind. He was a smart creature for a dog and fearless. I headed to the Montford District with its crooked streets. Its graveyard was a beacon for the ghosts of Asheville. Its geographic coordinates were calculated by Frederick Olmsted, the genius who constructed the landscaping at the Biltmore Estate. The Vanderbilts were steeped in the supernatural pursuits. Olmsted was their architect of the conduit to the spirit world. They searched the four corners of the earth, acquiring exotic plants and trees. Spirit trees from Ireland, holy trees from the dark continent, bamboos from the orient, all to bring the magic from those places to the Biltmore Forest and to Asheville. The Montford graveyard was at the epicenter of that conduit. The lieutenant would be waiting for me there. I arrived early afternoon. I was tired. It had been a long walk. The cemetery was empty except for a few lost souls. I leaped on top of a headstone. I bent over to read the name MORDECAI ALABASTER. I waited for dusk. It seemed a cliché, but spirits truly like to travel from twilight to dawn. Not that they'd be seen in the daylight but because the daylight reminds them of their life on earth. The warmth they will never feel again. That was true for all ghosts. But the lieutenant was not a ghost. He had never felt the warmth of the sun, for he was pure evil. The sun melted past the Blue Ridge Mountains. I had no fear. I felt almost relieved that this day had come. I had lived it often enough in my dreams. That feeling of standing on the edge of a great precipice and jumping off. The fear of falling is worse than the actual fall. I wanted to jump off into this last journey. I smelled the lieutenant as his wagon drifted through the headstones. There was one other ghost with him. He was not the one I had felt in the Biltmore basement. The lieutenant was holding a brass urn. "You can let him go," I said. "I'll show you the way."

He opened the urn and threw the ashes into the air. They swirled like a whirlwind and formed into Albert who looked at me with terror in his eyes. Then he disappeared.

I led the lieutenant out of Asheville onto the road that Agatha Hollows and I had traveled so long ago. Time slipped away as we walked all the way to Saluda, to the Green River. It was swollen from the spring rains. The lieutenant stopped on the muddy bank.

"You know I can't cross moving water. You've tried to deceive me. All your companions are dead." The lieutenant lashed out his whip, tearing fur and flesh from my back. I howled in pain.

"Wait," I said. "This is the only way to get where you want to go. You must follow the exact route that Agatha and I took. It's an intricate puzzle of connecting pieces you must pass through. I watched her closely. I know all the windows you must climb through before you can open the door. I can help you cross. There is magic I know that can give you your flesh back long enough to cross."

"If you fail me, Terra Rowan, your companions will suffer a painful death in this life and the next."

Agatha Hollows left behind crumbs of magic along our path, knowing that someday I would return and might need them. I couldn't summon magic in my form as a cat, but I could use hers. I followed the crumbs until I found the mountain laurel she had charmed. "Touch this tree," I said.

They touched the tree. The roots snapped out of the ground and wrapped around them. There was a loud humming from its trunk like a buzz saw. Flesh creeped across their bodies. In a matter of minutes, they stood in front of me as their former selves, the men I had seen in Agatha Hollows's cabin when they came for her. The mountain laurel withered, leaving nothing but a small sliver stuck in my paw. I tried to pull it out, but it was lodged too deep.

"Carry me, the water is too deep for me to cross," I told them.

The lieutenant picked me up and carried me toward the water. He stopped. "Walk. It's the only way," I said. As he stepped into the water, stepping-stones rose up to meet his feet. As the water rushed past us, we reached the middle of the river. This was where

Agatha Hollows warned me the bottom dropped off, deep and dark. I thought at that time she was warning me to be careful, but I knew now she was giving me a way to stop anyone who came after her. I reached up and sunk both my claws into his cheeks. He screamed in agony. The stepping-stones sunk back under the water. A Dullahan is two creatures—the head controls the body. Without it the creature will perish in the flesh and in its spirit. Agatha Hollows could not take his head at the bridge. She left that for me to do. I tugged until his head separated. His arms swayed madly, reaching for his head. He struggled as we sank to the bottom. I gave up my life to save my friends. I could feel my light struggling to pass from my body as I exhausted all my air. I welcomed this death and awaited my new life. And then I felt myself being lifted out of the water. A large black bear had grabbed the lieutenant's head and was dragging him and me to the shore. The bear tore at the head as the lieutenant's body pounded at it. The spell wore off in time for him to grab his head and turn back into a vapor, disappearing into the woods. I lay nearly dead at the feet of the black bear. I could smell its foul stench. I was waiting for it to finish me. Instead, it picked me up and stared into my eyes as it shape-shifted into the form of Mrs. Lund.

"Terra, are you okay?" she asked.

I was too weak to answer.

She built a fire and laid me close to warm me. She watched over me throughout the night. In the morning, I woke as she was turning a trout on a stick over the fire. She took off pieces and fed them to me. I could feel my strength returning.

We finished the fish. I sat up and studied her. I had never met a shape-shifter before. Elizabeth had told me of the ancient days when they walked with witches. Not quite friends but not enemies. They had a mutual respect for each other's magic. Somewhere in our great history we might actually have shared the same bloodline. The magic we had woken in Asheville roused her from whatever slumber she had kept.

"That's right, Terra, I was drawn to your magic," she said, putting out the fire.

"You can read my thoughts. I wasn't speaking to you."

"Yes, Terra. When Abigail Oakhaven found her spirit tree, it awoke white and black magic. It woke the Dullahan which lay dormant after Agatha Hollows took his flesh." She threw water on the fire, poked at the embers. "It joined the gray coats to hunt witches to drain their light. When it found Agatha Hollows, it made its way to the eternal light. Now we're both searching for the same thing to reach the next level of our powers, to follow Agatha Hollows into the light. We can't let him do that, can we?"

"That's why you contacted Mrs. Loblolly. You knew her ancestor, the colonel, was tasked with finding supernatural powers to fight the war. You knew that if you followed her you would find the lieutenant."

"The colonel was sent a message from a private under the lieutenant's command. The message read they found a witch with great powers and that they had followed her to Poinsett Bridge," Mrs. Lund said. "When the colonel and his men arrived at the bridge, they found the lieutenant and his men reduced to ashes, their uniforms intact. The colonel kept the uniforms and the ashes and locked them away, thinking they were killed by magic, which they were. Agatha Hollows reached out from the portal just long enough to destroy them, but the Dullahan did not die a true death. The spirit lived on trapped in the ashes, dormant until you woke it. You woke me also, and I've been hunting the hunter. I contacted Mrs. Loblolly, and she told me she had the colonel's collection of Civil War uniforms. When I found the lieutenant's uniform, it still had remnants of his ashes. I placed it on the mannequin in the Biltmore along with the colonel's sword to draw him to me. It thought it killed me before I could kill it. It doesn't know the limitations of witches and shape-shifters. It doesn't know how to kill me. Your friends aren't safe. You need to go back and warn them." With that, she turned into a great horned owl and lifted me up gently in her talons. She could have made me take her to Dark Corner to the portal, but instead she brought me back to Asheville. For now, I believed she was a good being, a kind being, and that's the way I would proceed with her.

She dropped me at the doorstep of the Tangledwood Estate. "Save your friends, Terra," she said before flying up over the mountain ridge.

"Terra back." Pixel flew on top of me. "You keep promise, Terra. Good Terra." He was so excited to see me he didn't notice Mrs. Lund. For now, I would keep that secret to myself.

Mrs. Twiggs, Abigail, and Charlotte came out and joined the celebration. Even Tracker acted glad to see me as he cleaned my fur.
Albert stood quietly on the corner of the great steps.

"Thank you, Terra, for bringing Albert back. But what about the
lieutenant? What happened?" Mrs. Twiggs asked.

"He'll be back, but we'll be ready. Gather the ladies. I have a
story to tell."

GET A CLUE

I WOKE WITH A START. ABIGAIL peered into my room. "Did you hear that scream, Terra?"

I nodded as we ran down the long hallway of the second floor of the Tangledwood Estate. The ladies gathered in the hallway outside their bedroom doors. The late-night story of my adventures had kept the ladies up all night. They had agreed to stay at the estate. There is safety in numbers, and I felt evil brewing, so I knew we needed to rely on each other.

We ran down the long, spiral staircase. Abigail stumbled at the bottom of the stairs as we heard another scream. Mrs. Twiggs flipped on the foyer light. We followed the echo of the scream into the library. We found Charlotte standing over the lifeless body of Miss Hartwell. A stream of blood flowed from her head wound, and a silver candlestick lay next to her, covered in blood. Mrs. Twiggs felt for a pulse but shook her head. Miss Hartwell was gone.

The ladies gathered around in a circle, all talking at once. I saw Mr. Tangledwood puffing his pipe from the easy chair by the wall of bookcases. He uncrossed his legs, stood up, and floated off through the wall. Mrs. Twiggs grabbed an afghan off the couch and placed it respectively over Miss Hartwell.

Charlotte shook uncontrollably. Unlike the rest of us she had never seen a dead body. Abigail took her into the kitchen. I walked around the body slowly, sniffing for clues. The rug was well traveled by the rest of the ladies leaving their scent. I looked up at their faces. They had become hardened war-torn warriors. Not from lack of compassion but because they knew the big picture and what was coming. I heard their thoughts. Who did this? Who's next? How do we stop this? And most importantly, why?

The paramedics arrived before the police. A short while later Detective Willows came in, notepad in hand. He lifted the afghan off Miss Hartwell and peeled it back slowly so he could examine the wound. He motioned to the young officers to rope off the area. "Please all of you wait in the next room." He motioned to us.

The crime scene team crawled around the library like a bunch of angry ants, rubber gloved, lifting, examining, taking pictures. Detective Willows donned his reassuring smile. We all sat in the sitting room, silent. We noticed Charlotte crying and shaking. Detective Willows sat down next to her and put his arm around her. "Are you okay, dear? Do you need medical attention?"

She shook her head.

Mrs. Twiggs spoke. "Detective, her screams woke us. We were all asleep on the second floor."

"Did anybody see anything? Or anyone?"

"No," the ladies answered in unison.

"Charlotte, why were you in the library?" Detective Willows asked.

"I couldn't sleep. I came down to get something to read. That's when I... I found her."

The detective stepped over to the front door, examining the lock and the catch plate. I followed him to take a closer look. I had noticed the door had been slightly ajar when we found Miss Hartwell. He thought the same as I did that it was forced open, not an easy feat. He ran his gloved finger along the edge of the door, catching it on a sliver. A young officer came up behind him. Mrs.

Twiggs walked over.

"Butch, what's going on?"

"Beatrice, the door was forced open. Is there anything missing in the house?"

"I don't know. We didn't think to check."

I searched the house for anything out of place. Mrs. Tangled-wood kept a tidy home. The estate sale left the house with the essentials, bedding, and furniture. All items to help stage the home for sale. Mrs. Twiggs joined me taking inventory using the ledger from the estate sale.

"All here, Terra," she said. "Maybe the robber was interrupted by Miss Hartwell before he could steal anything."

I thought for a moment. "We didn't check the Not For Sale room, Mrs. Twiggs." We hurried to the den behind the library. We found family photo albums and other boxes of personal items.

"The painting, Terra, the one Emma left for Charlotte is gone."

Mrs. Twiggs made tea as the detectives interviewed each lady. We watched as the paramedics took Miss Hartwell away.

Mrs. Twiggs called Detective Willows into the room. "As far as we can tell the only thing missing is an oil landscape of a field of flowers near Poinsett Bridge. It was Emma's favorite. It was a gift to the Tangledwoods some years ago from George Vanderbilt. She treasured that painting. She wanted to keep it in her family." Mrs. Twiggs ran over to the writing table and opened the drawer. She retrieved a business card and gave it to the detective. "Here, Darren White, this man was here the day of the estate sale asking about the painting. I told him it wasn't available. He seemed very interested in it and upset when I told him it was not for sale."

Detective Willows took the card, snapping it between his fingers. He stared at the name. "Mr. Not Mrs., huh?" he mumbled.

"Butch, what are you talking about?"

"Sorry, Beatrice. Mr. White with a candlestick in the library. I couldn't help myself."

Mrs. Twiggs was not amused.

"Sorry, Beatrice, it's been a long day."

After the police left, Mrs. Loblolly spoke up. "Beatrice, was this the lieutenant?"

"I don't think so, June. Miss Hartwell was human. She didn't have anything that the lieutenant wanted."

"If it wasn't the lieutenant, then who?" Mrs. Loblolly asked.

"Why did they take the painting?" Mrs. Stickman asked.

Mrs. Twiggs looked down at me. I leaped onto the end table. "George Vanderbilt believed in the magic of these woods, so if he did commission that painting, he understood the power of Poinsett Bridge," I said.

"Emma's had that painting in her family for generations. Wouldn't you think if there were some magic in it, Emma would have known?"

"Not necessarily. Mrs. Tangledwood just discovered her powers right before she was killed," I said. "Magic can lay dormant for hundreds even thousands of years waiting for its master to awaken it." I thought of Mrs. Lund and the other creatures that had awakened since Halloween.

"That painting was given to Emma's grandmother after George Vanderbilt died. He meant for it to go to the Tangledwoods to protect it. The Tangledwoods shared his belief in the supernatural," Mrs. Twiggs said. "Terra, what is the power of Poinsett Bridge? Why did the lieutenant want you to take him there?"

I had kept that part of the story from the ladies. It was a secret reserved for higher beings, but I felt it time and they had a right to know. "Mrs. Twiggs, Poinsett Bridge is a portal to other realms. When a witch walks through, she becomes a stronger version of herself but risks the danger of being stuck in another realm. The same is true for dark creatures. They become more powerful and more evil."

The ladies were silent, absorbing what I said. "Terra, what if you were to walk through the portal?" Abigail asked.

"I tried once before. I wasn't allowed entry." I turned my back and started cleaning myself.

"We can't let the lieutenant through the portal," all the ladies shouted.

"The way to the portal is a labyrinth. Agatha Hollows could see the path and led me along it. To anyone not on the path it appears as merely a bridge. The path runs along a corridor from Asheville to Dark Corner, South Carolina. As you follow the path, you gather magic to complete the puzzle. If you stray from that path even by a step the portal will be locked to your entry. The lieutenant knows this. He can't reach the portal without me to lead him, and that's why none of you are safe as long as I am with you."

"Terra, take me to the portal," Abigail said.

"I can't remember the way. I made it as far as the Green River. My intention was never to cross, but even if I had crossed, the rest of the path is so intricate with twists and turns I will never find it."

Pixel pranced into the room, knocking me over onto my back. He stood over me. "No, Terra," he said with a stern voice. "Not again. Terra and Pixel go Terra, say right?"

"Yes, Pixel."

The ladies circled around me and joined hands. "No, Terra, where you go, we go." Their eyes became fiery red; they meditated and became their witch goddesses, their true light shining like a beacon from within them. The room became a swirling dervish. I felt dizzy. I couldn't breathe, and then like Dorothy caught in the tornado, everything stopped dead. I looked around the circle, stopping when I saw Charlotte. Abigail stood in the center with her hands raised to the ceiling. Charlotte completed the circle, Pixel wrapped around her neck. He was terrified. I had never seen the coven unite their powers like that before. I stared at Charlotte with deep intensity. I knew she couldn't hear me, but she stared back at me. Was she our ninth Wiccan? She was a Tangledwood, meaning that Emma's blood ran through her. Why hadn't I seen it before? Pixel leaped from around her neck. Abigail saw what I had seen. A big smile grew on her face.

"You have to make sure, Abigail." All the ladies turned to stare at Charlotte.

"What, what are you all looking at? That was awesome. Can we do it again?" Charlotte asked.

CHARLOTTE'S
SECOND CHANCE

MRS. TWIGGS BUSTLED INTO THE kitchen and prepared the special turning potion.

"You completed the circle, Charlotte."

"But I'm not a Wiccan. I drank the potion. Nothing happened."

"The same thing happened to Mrs. Twiggs. Black magic kept her from turning at first," I said. "It might have done the same to you."

Abigail walked Charlotte over to the couch and sat down next to her while Mrs. Stickman lit the fire. There was an air of anticipation.

Mrs. Twiggs returned, carrying a teacup. Steam rose from its brim. She placed it down on the coffee table in front of Charlotte. "Okay, dear, drink it up."

Charlotte lowered her head and sniffed the concoction and then grimaced. "It smells worse than before."

Mrs. Twiggs said, "Drink it quickly."

Charlotte raised the cup, looked at Abigail, and then downed it. I waited for something, anything, that would transform her. There was still nothing. No puff of smoke, nothing. Her aura colors did not change. She looked human. I could hear a collective sigh.

Charlotte said, "So what happens now? Do I get a broom? Do I grow warts?"

Abigail laughed. "No, Char, it didn't work. I'm afraid you're human."

"You don't have to say it like that, Abigail. Like it's a bad thing."

"Oh no, it's not bad. It's just we had hoped you would close the coven. We need nine. I'm a witch. I can't close the coven. It has to be nine members of equal powers. The same but different. Think of it like all the ladies are double AA batteries and I'm a D battery. When they hold hands and form the circle, those batteries combine to make a more powerful charge. If I were to try to complete that circle, it would short-circuit everything. I've never seen their circle that powerful. We thought you were the missing battery. We all have power, but we can't mix and match."

Charlotte nodded. "I'm sorry to disappoint everyone."

MRS. TWIGGS
GOES TO JAIL

M RS. TWIGGS HUNG UP THE phone. "That was Detective Willows. They arrested Mr. White."

"We have to talk to him and find out why that painting is so important," I told her.

Mrs. Twiggs and I left for the police station. I scratched at my emotional support animal vest. She looked over at me while she was driving and smiled. "I know, Terra, it's annoying, but it's the only way to get you in the door."

She carried me into the station and walked up to the desk sergeant. "Detective Willows is expecting me. Beatrice Twiggs."

He picked up a phone and called the detective, who arrived shortly from the back office. "Let's walk in here so we can talk," Detective Willows said.

Mrs. Twiggs followed, carrying me and petting my fur. We all sat down at a small room off the main hallway, which was lined with small offices.

"Beatrice, why do you need to talk to Mr. White?"

"The painting was very important to Emma, and she wanted Charlotte to have it."

"We didn't find the painting. He's insisting he's innocent," Detective Willows said, tilting back in the chair, which squeaked in protest. "He does have a record of breaking and entering. That's the only reason I could hold him."

"I need to ask him why the painting was so important. I need to understand why it was worth killing Miss Hartwell. If for nothing else for Emma's sake. Miss Hartwell was a devoted companion and nurse to Emma. She took care of her as her health declined."

"Five minutes, Beatrice, I can only give you five minutes." He let us into a room full of holding cells. Mr. White sat by himself on a metal stool, staring at us. The rest of the room was empty. Detective Willows pulled up a chair, placing it directly in front of the cell for Mrs. Twiggs. "Five minutes," he said again as he left the room.

"Mrs. Twiggs," Darren White said, standing. "We met at the estate sale."

"Yes," she replied.

"I want you to know I'm innocent. I would never harm a soul."

As he spoke, I felt the same sensation as when I first saw Mr. White. A shadow of a feeling but now I realized it wasn't him causing the shadow. It was the subject, the painting. I could feel his strong desire for it. He was drawn to it.

"Why did you come for the painting?" Mrs. Twiggs asked him.

"It's quite valuable. It was a gift from George Vanderbilt to the Tangledwoods."

"It's more than that, isn't it?" she persisted.

He walked up closer, placing his hands on the bars. As he did, Beatrice grabbed them. His body shook. "Tell me the truth," she said.

His eyes darted around the room. "I'm innocent," he said.

"Tell me the truth," she repeated.

"I'm innocent."

"Mrs. Twiggs," I shouted. "He's telling the truth."

"It's true. There are witches in Asheville. George Vanderbilt was right." He said through his tears.

"Tell me about the painting," Mrs. Twiggs said.

"It's a map to a magic doorway."

She let go of his hands, and he fell to the floor. He stood up slowly and rubbed his hands. His eyes were full of fear. "You are a witch. How did you do that?"

Beatrice stood up. He cowed back in terror. "How does the painting work?"

"I don't know. I just know the history of the painting. I studied the art of the Vanderbilt's. I thought it was a myth; the story makes the painting more valuable to collectors. But now I know it's real."

"He's telling the truth, Beatrice, he didn't kill Miss Hartwell," I told her.

She waved her hand in the air, and Mr. White collapsed on the metal bunk. She said one word, "Forget." And then we left.

Detective Willows opened the door leading back out to the free world, staring at Mrs. Twiggs. She raised her hand. He grabbed it by the wrist. "Don't Beatrice. I don't want to forget what I just saw." She lowered her hand as he let go. "I'll help you anyway I can." He gave her a hug.

We rode back to the Tangledwood Estate, mostly in silence, as I cleaned my fur. It was a nervous tic I had picked up over the past century or so. Mrs. Twiggs drove into the Montford District and stopped the car when she reached Karen Owen's home. I leaped out of the car and followed her up the steps, looking left and right over the wraparound porch for the rocking chair man. Thankfully the chair was empty. Mrs. Twiggs lightly tapped the gold door knocker. Squirrel appeared from around the deck. Mrs. Owen opened the door and welcomed us in. She led us into the front room. Mrs. Twiggs settled on the couch, Mrs. Owen across from her on the high-back chair like a queen on her throne I thought.

"Karen, I know I'm in debt to you, but I need to ask you a favor," Mrs. Twiggs said.

Mrs. Owen smiled. She said, "Beatrice you've accumulated quite a tab. I think it's time we talked about payment."

"Of course, Karen, what do I owe you?"

Mrs. Owen looked at the end of the couch directly at me.

Mrs. Twiggs appeared confused.

"I require the cat."

"Karen, you must be joking."

Mrs. Owen shook her head. "Terra Rowan was a very powerful witch in her previous form. I have the means to extract those powers."

"What do you mean extract?"

"Don't worry, Beatrice. It won't harm her. And the powers are of no use to her in her present form."

"What will happen to her?"

"She will live out the rest of her day as a cat not able to communicate. Not tied to her past or headed toward her future. She will live a normal cat life and die a normal cat life. She will be joyfully bliss in her ignorance."

I extracted my claws and hissed. Squirrel pounced on me and knocked me off the couch. I turned and screamed into Squirrel's mind. "Get out." She bounced off the floor and ran out screaming. I jumped on the coffee table.

"Mrs. Owen, I know the tab you keep. We will find a fair payment for Mrs. Twiggs's bill," I said.

She lifted me by my scruff and brought me close. "I can take away all your pain, Terra Rowan. The memories that haunt you. I can give you peace."

Mrs. Twiggs clutched the silver amulet from Agatha Hollows. "Karen, the price is too high." She raised her hand.

"No," I said. Karen Owen was much too powerful a being for Mrs. Twiggs to confront. "I will lead you to the portal, Mrs. Owen. I will show you how to enter. I know Agatha Hollows shut your way."

She put me back down onto the coffee table and reached under the seat, pulling out a leather-bound book. She opened it and then handed Mrs. Twiggs a fountain pen. "Prick your finger, Beatrice, with this pen." Beatrice did as she requested. The pen soaked up Mrs. Twiggs's blood. "Sign here." Beatrice examined her bill and signed. Mrs. Owen snapped the book shut. "Now how may I help you?"

"We have questions about a painting."

"I know which painting you refer to," Mrs. Owen said. "The road into Dark Corner. George Vanderbilt commissioned that painting. At one of the séances they held, the dead spoke of the trail to Poinsett Bridge. The painting is charmed as it was painted by one of the last wood fairies. She was brought to the forest by Olmsted from one of his excursions to Ireland. Her kind have passed, but the magic of the painting carries on, but it's only part of the map." She looked down at me. "You know the rest, don't you? You know how to get to the river."

PIXEL'S MISSING

"PIXEL," I SCREAMED AS I roamed the halls of the Tangled-wood Estate. He had been acting so strange, but it was not like him to miss a meal or two or three. But now it had been nearly two days since I had seen him. I entered the library. Mr. Tangled-wood sat by the fire, puffing on his pipe. He had passed several years before Mrs. Tangledwood. Unlike Albert Twiggs, he lingered not for the love of his wife but for the love of his possessions. He stood guard over them like a night watchman at the Louvre. His cars, his books, all called to him. Mrs. Tangledwood had only spoken of him once, and it was not fondly. He was a selfish man in life and continued to be selfish in death. "Mr. Tangledwood where is my friend? Where is the orange cat?"

He ignored me and stared onto the lawn, puffing away. He took out a pipe cleaner and scraped the bowl. I extended one claw and stuck it deep into the leather of his chair, ripping it open. He gasped and stared at me. Then he smiled and packed his bowl with tobacco. I leaped onto a table and knocked over a Ming vase. This time he ignored me. I saw him staring out at the open garage door. I ran out and leaped onto the hood of the 1961 Mercedes. He floated in the corner of the garage, watching. I extended my claw and scratched the hood. He flew down, eyes wide open, screaming at me, but nothing came out. I went into the front seat and tore it apart.

"Stop," he yelled. "Stop."

"You can speak, can't you?"

"Stop, you filthy creature."

"Where's my friend? Did the lieutenant take him?"

"No," he shouted.

I raised my claw about to scratch the dash.

"Stop. I don't know where your friend is."

And then I realized Mr. Tangledwood was a spy. "Tell me about the lieutenant," I commanded as I gently rubbed my claw along the dashboard.

"The lieutenant is gathering an army. He's going to destroy you and all the other filthy witches."

"You have been spying for him, haven't you?"

"He promised me I could stay on my estate and live here forever. I want no part of the war that's coming. I want to be left alone."

I could see he was a worthless creature. He had no fight in this battle. He took no side other than his own. I ran onto the front lawn. It would be dark soon, another night with no Pixel. The end of another day without Pixel. I could feel he was still alive. I could smell his aura. It seemed close. I lay on my back, staring up at the clouds, imitating Pixel rolling back and forth, thinking of the simplicity of his happiness. The little things that gave him joy. Anger rose inside me. The thought of any harm coming to him made me want to do harm. I closed my eyes and called out to him. Then I felt something land on my belly. I opened my eyes to see the purple-and-white butterfly that had followed Pixel around. Pixel's friend, Flutter, as he named her. She flew and circled me. I followed her back to the estate, back inside the grand hall with its marble floor and high ceiling. She floated into the library, land-ing on a book. It was Emma's favorite book, the first edition of a collection of writings by Frederick Law Olmsted. I reached up to look at it. As I pulled it down, a wall of books opened up, revealing a secret room. An orange blur leaped out on top of me.

"Hungry. Me so hungry," he said, biting my neck.

"Pixel?"

"Terra me eat first."

The french doors leading into the library slammed shut. Charlotte stared down at us.

"You know, don't you? You can tell the others." She grabbed the fireplace poker, lifting it over her head. I was in shock, unable to move. Before it crushed my skull, Pixel leaped, pushing me out of the way. The poker landed its blow across his back. I regained my senses and leaped onto her, clawing at her neck and face. She screamed. The doors burst open.

Mrs. Twiggs screamed, "Terra, what are you doing?" She saw Pixel broken and bloody on the floor and looked at Charlotte, poker still in her hand. Mrs. Twiggs raised her palms and cast a spell. The poker fell from Charlotte's hand, and she stood frozen in time. Mrs. Twiggs knelt next to Pixel, listening for his heartbeat. "It's very faint, Terra."

Abigail ran into the room, not understanding what she was seeing. She knelt down beside Pixel, sobs coming. Mrs. Twiggs lifted his limp body. As we drove to the animal hospital, Abigail incited every healing spell she had learned. Nothing was working. Pixel remained still, unmoving. He was too far gone. Abigail had once saved Tracker from near death, but this was different. This was sudden and fatal. My tears merged with Abigail's. Pixel's aura was a shadow. He was leaving this world. I could see him struggling to open his eyes. My heart wrenched from my body. I screamed out. He had given his life for mine. We reached the animal hospital where the technicians rushed him to surgery. Already the other ladies were arriving. They stood vigil in the waiting room, each one praying to their ancestors and to the true and only one Goddess. They held hands in their circle, but the powerful magic was not there. I realized then it wasn't Charlotte that completed the circuitry of the coven, it was Pixel. She had been holding Pixel. He was the conduit. Something or someone had gifted the magic to Pixel. I prayed that magic would see him through now. I noticed a bloodhound in the waiting room with no master, collar, or leash.

"Mrs. Lund," I whispered.

She nodded her head with long droopy ears flopping to and fro.

We walked outside. "Terra, they are gathering. All the dark souls are rallying around the lieutenant with the promise that he will lead them into the portal. All the lost souls that haunt the Poinsett Bridge are waiting to join him."

"I can't leave Pixel. I can't."

"The only way to save him is for you to enter the portal."

We waited out the night. In the morning the doctor joined us in the waiting room.

"My name is Dr. Courtney," he said to Mrs. Twiggs. "Your cat is very…"

"Pixel, his name is Pixel." Mrs. Twiggs interrupted.

"Yes, of course, Pixel, he has a broken spine. I did what I could. The next twenty-four hours are critical. If he does recover, he'll never walk again."

Mrs. Twiggs cried into her handkerchief. Abigail put her arm around her.

"I'm so sorry. We have to wait and see," Dr. Courtney said before heading back the way he had come.

Mrs. Lund stared at me.

"Mrs. Twiggs, Abigail, we have to get back to the estate," I said. The ladies promised to remain with Pixel as the three of us headed back to the Tangledwood Estate.

The sun crashed through the stained-glass window of the library, engulfing Charlotte in its cranberry-red glow. She stood frozen as we had left her. The secret passageway door was ajar. The sliver of the light from the windows illuminated the missing painting. We entered gazing at the treasures there, Emma Tangledwood's stolen treasures. Mrs. Twiggs walked up to Charlotte and waved her hands. She collapsed, shaking her head.

"Who are you?" Mrs. Twiggs asked.

Before Charlotte could spew her lies, Mrs. Twiggs slid her finger across her lips. She screamed as they burned bright red. "My name is Morgan Andrews."

"Why did you pretend to be Charlotte Tangledwood?"

"I…" She began to stutter; her lips burned bright red.

"You can't lie."

"Stop, please. Miss Hartwell came to me at the Swannanoa Correctional Center for women. She was a nurse there before she came to work for Mrs. Tangledwood. She showed me a picture of a young girl, Charlotte. She said I looked like her. That I could make a lot of money pretending I was her."

"Why did you kill her?"

She tried keeping her lips shut, but they flew open. "She said I would inherit this mansion and all Mrs. Tangledwood's money. When we found out that all of it was going to the Biltmore Foundation except for that stupid painting, I told her I wanted a share of everything she had stolen. She had been taking things from the old woman for years, hiding it away. When she refused, I said I would tell the police. That night we got in an argument. She had a knife. She said she would kill me if I said anything. I grabbed the poker. I-I… It was self-defense. I didn't mean to kill her."

"And you hid the painting so you could blame Mr. White?"

"He was obsessed with the painting. He kept calling and texting me," she said.

"You made it look like he broke in?"

She struggled to open her lips and then said, "Yes, I panicked. I was afraid. I didn't want to go back to the prison. I saw Miss Hartwell sneaking stuff into that room. I saw her pull on that book. After I killed her, I hid the painting in there. Pixel saw me and followed me in."

Mrs. Twiggs touched Morgan on the shoulder, and she collapsed. Detective Willows was the first to arrive. Mrs. Twiggs sat across from him, sipping tea, filling him in on the whole story.

Abigail and I examined the painting. I couldn't believe it took me that long to realize what I was looking at. "Abigail, this is the same map Agatha Hollows used to get to Poinsett Bridge."

"It doesn't look like a map," Abigail said.

"No, but it is the same path to the bridge," I said. "It's enchanted. We have to decipher the secret to reveal it. Mrs. Tangledwood knew the spell. She wanted to leave the answer to her great-niece—the real Charlotte. This is Mrs. Tangledwood's greatest treasure. All her other possessions were earthly and will turn to dust in time. This is the true gift she left for her bloodline. Mrs. Twiggs," I said. "The book, the book that opens the secret room."

Mrs. Twiggs looked at me and ran to the shelf. She examined the spine and read out loud, "Humphrey Repton. *The Theory and Practice of Landscaping*. 1795. First edition." Mrs. Twiggs turned to us. "This is the book that inspired Olmsted to become a landscape architect. He used this book to teach his pupils. He said, 'You are to read this seriously as a law student would read Blackstone.' Emma knew that the Ladies of the Biltmore Society would know this reference. She wants us to read Olmsted's personal journal and to read it seriously." Mrs. Twiggs checked the shelves but couldn't find it. She went into the secret room, checking the drawers in the writing desk. They were locked. "Open," she said, and the drawers flung open. She found Frederick Law Olmsted's personal journal—the one that George Vanderbilt gifted to the Tangledwoods. She brought it to us. "Emma told me about the journal but she never let me read it."

Abigail took the book, flipping through it, running a finger along the lines. "Terra, there's a passage here about his trip to Ireland to bring saplings to the Biltmore Forest. He mentions oak, ash, and thorn. He brought a clipping of an ancient oak tree. He's talking about my spirit oak tree, isn't he?"

I nodded.

Abigail continued reading. "He mentioned traveling into the hedges of Lullymore in the County Kildare. The locals told him of a single hawthorn tree that was said to be the home of the last woodland fairy. Intrigued by the fairy tale, Olmsted brought the hawthorn tree to Biltmore Forest." Abigail closed the journal. "That's all that's in there, Terra."

"We are to read that journal as the letter of the law. I believe that Olmsted brought with him the last fairy on earth. She kept the secret of the portal at Poinsett Bridge. Agatha Hollows knew how to open it and showed me the labyrinth to follow to reach the river, to gather the magic to cross over, but she did not show me how to continue. That way I could never be held hostage to black magic and deliver them into the portal. This painting is a map, painted by the last fairy of Lullymore, the last fairy on earth. She only gave Olmsted half the puzzle. Agatha gave me the other half."

"We have to go," Abigail said.

"But, Abigail, no one has ever come back. I didn't tell you this, but I saw Elizabeth in the portal. She couldn't leave it. She couldn't cross back into this world."

"I don't care, Terra, we have to save Pixel. We have to defend ourselves against the lieutenant. How do we decipher the map?"

"Like the Wiccans, the fairies' bloodlines faded as the magic of this world faded and the humans took over, encroaching on their land. Their magic dwindled as the human science became the new magic. In 1820 when the Poinsett Bridge was built to connect the Carolinas, the fairies used the last of their magic and the magic of these ancient mountains to open the portal to the fairy world from where they first came. They hoped that one day they could return to our world which they loved. The Lullymore fairy was the last to cross over. The rest had already evolved."

"Evolved into what?" Abigail asked.

"Butterflies," I said.

We turned when we heard a thud against the window. Flutter landed on the windowsill. I paused and stared. "There wasn't enough magic left for them to save their race. Elizabeth told me this story a long time ago. I thought it was literally a fairy tale. She told me so many fairy tales when I was a little girl. She said only the fairy queen could enter the portal and return the fairies to the woods."

FLUTTER

MRS. TWIGGS FINISHED WITH DETECTIVE Willows and then came over to us. "Detective Willows is trying to find the real Charlotte. Her parents died several years ago, and there has been no trace of her since then. They're releasing Mr. White."

Flutter pounded against the window again. The three of us went outside and watched as she danced from one hibiscus to another, yellow to apricot to orange and then back. It took me several minutes to realize there was a pattern to her dance. I ran back to study the painting and saw the same colors. There was a path, a dance of the fairies to make the tumblers click to unlock the portal.

Abigail filled her backpack with supplies. Mrs. Twiggs drove us to the animal hospital so we could say our goodbyes to the ladies. They all remained glued to Pixel's side. I stared down at my friend, my familiar. He lay still, monitors and IVs hooked up to his tattered and broken body. Flutter flew around the room, landing next to Pixel. She flapped her wings fiercely, and a small sprinkle of dust flew off them, covering Pixel. He moaned and then opened one eye for a second, staring at me before closing it again. It was late at night, the best time to travel. We'd have to follow the stars to make our way to the river. Abigail picked me up, cradling me in her arms.

Mrs. Twiggs pulled us aside. "We're all coming with you," she said. "We've trained for this day."

"It's better if we travel light and unnoticed, and you need to stay with Pixel. I don't want to leave him alone," I said although I would welcome their presence.

"We can't let you go alone. The two of you aren't prepared to fight this battle on your own," Mrs. Twiggs argued.

It saddened me to say, but Mrs. Twiggs needed to hear the truth. All the ladies needed to hear the truth. They gathered around me, all in a semicircle. "We only have one chance to defeat the darkness and that is for Abigail to enter the portal. There's just too many, and they are too powerful. We can't fight them and survive. Some of you would perish on the trail. I can't let that happen. If we fall, you will be the last defense of Asheville."

"Very well, Terra," Mrs. Twiggs said.

The ladies laid their hands on Abigail, offering what they could from their magic to protect us. Mrs. Raintree sang a Cherokee blessing; Mrs. Birchbark held Abigail's hand. Her goddess mother Kuan Yin eased Abigail's suffering for Abigail's heart was broken.

Mrs. Stickman ran outside, and with a wave of her hand, the dark clouds disappeared, filling the sky with stars. She turned to Abigail. "To help light your way," she said with a smile.

Mrs. Branchworthy placed a small stone in Abigail's hand. Abigail stared at it, knowing she could make her own fire, but Mrs. Branchworthy said, "You'll know what to do and when to use this." She put the stone in the front flap of her backpack.

Mrs. Bartlett handed Abigail her silver knife. Abigail slid it into her boot. Mrs. Bowers', descendant of Rhiannon, Queen Witch, said, "I've been summoning the magic of the wee ones." As she spoke, a dragonfly flew into the room and landed on Abigail's shoulder. Abigail smiled and put her finger up to the dragonfly. It climbed onto it, a beautiful fluorescent blue with iridescent flapping wings. "If you need us, send the dragonfly," she said.

Mrs. Loblolly handed Abigail a compass, a very old and battered one. "This will help you find your way home. It doesn't point north. It points to your loved ones. It's drawn to our love for you, so you will always find us," she said.

Mrs. Twiggs reached in her cloak and pulled out an apophyllite pendant like the one she had given Detective Willows. She put it around Abigail's neck and whispered an incantation in a language I didn't recognize. "Take care," she then said.

We turned back for one last glance at Pixel. Tracker sat, staring at Pixel and let out a mournful howl. Then he turned and followed us out. He would not leave Abigail's side.

We left without looking back. After several hours of walking from downtown Asheville to the outskirts of Hendersonville, Abigail sat on a park bench. "Terra, I can summon a car or motorcycle or plane. Why do we have to walk? There's no time."

"This is the way Agatha Hollows found the portal." I gazed at the stars. "Each step we take down her path unlocks her magic." I questioned myself the whole time we walked. Could we do this? I was a cat, Abigail a mere girl. I had made it to the river with the lieutenant and had just enough magic to turn him to flesh. I thought of what waited in the water for those on this journey without the magic to cross. We continued our trek keeping to the woods. By the end of the first day, we camped on the bank of the Green River. Abigail gathered firewood. She took a can of beans and heated it over the flame. I walked along the bank, staring at the water rushing by and thought about the lieutenant. I could feel his new skin under my claws. Agatha Hollows had cast a spell that lowered the river and raised stepping-stones so we could walk across. I didn't remember that spell. I tried for years to remember the exact words she spoke, but they were jumbled in my head. The stones retracted when I crossed with the lieutenant. Flutter landed on my back. She tried to speak to me. I knew she was talking, but I couldn't understand her. I had never tried speaking to creatures of her kind. I spoke with cats and dogs, squirrels but never insects. I thought them beneath me. How proud was I? Me, a cat—no a witch cat. Whatever Flutter was now, she still had traces of her ancient magic running through her blood. She had drained all her powers on Pixel. She was the reason that Pixel had premonitions, that Pixel united the coven circle. Now the color had gone from her wings, faded. She looked pale and sickly. Like my dear friend

Pixel, she was dying.

Abigail handed me a plate. I ate around the beans, chewing on the pork. She took out her phone, examining the picture of the painting. "Terra, what are the chances that these flowers painted over a hundred years ago are still growing wild?"

I said, "They're enchanted, Abigail. They will be there." I said half believing myself. Mankind had stomped all over this earth, bringing their devastation, their machines, their pollution. I closed my eyes and nestled up to Abigail. She pulled the blanket up tight, a cool spring night. The fire felt comforting; the owls sang us to sleep. The owls that Mrs. Birchbark sent to watch over us. I had seen Mrs. Lund following far behind us, watching over her shoulder. She had kept the form of the bloodhound so she could follow our scent without giving us away to whichever of the lieutenant's minions followed us.

"Terra, wake up," Abigail whispered. I opened my eyes. It was still dark. I focused into the woods. I saw dozens of red eyes staring out at us. Tracker stood at attention, emitting a low growl. The first creature stepped slowly into the clearing. It was the size and shape of a coyote, but it was without fur. Its skin was the color of mud, and it smelled rancid. It let out a low, deep growl. Tracker answered back, lunging toward it, baring his teeth. The others crawled out of the woods and surrounded us. Abigail grabbed the stone from her backpack. It glowed red hot. She held it high, and fireballs shot out engulfing the hounds. The leader backed up. She raised her hand and spoke "Back into the dark I send you." The creatures yelped in pain and stepped slowly back into the woods except for one. It wriggled in pain as its body jerked. Its bones cracked as it grew twice its size. Abigail repeated, "Back into the dark, I send you." The creature inched its way forward toward Abigail until it was just a few feet in front of us. Abigail grabbed the silver blade from her boot and stabbed at its face. The creature grabbed the blade and threw it to the side. "Terra, I can't stop this creature. What is it?"

"The humans call it a hellhound." I thought about how Agatha Hollows had killed a similar beast, but before I could tell Abigail, it lunged at her. She waved her hand, sending it tumbling into the water. It jumped out and headed back toward her. From out of the woods, the bloodhound ran out. Tracker and Mrs. Lund bit and tore at its rancid flesh. Agatha Hollows's dogs had killed a beast like this. They were bred to be immune to the poison of its bite. Descendant of the dogs that walked beside the earth walkers, millions of years before the humans, Tracker chased the hound into the woods. Abigail watched through Tracker's eyes as he killed each beast one by one. Mrs. Lund lay with her side wide open in the form of the bloodhound, then she shifted into her real self. The black veins of poison twisted around her body from the wounds. Abigail ran to her, pressing her hands against her wounds, trying to stop the bleeding.

Mrs. Lund smiled. "This is me, Abigail." She was a beautiful elf-like creature, slender with white-blond hair the color of Abigail's, her eyes, the color of milky-blue opals. "The lieutenant is waiting at the bridge. I kept him off your trail. He can't enter the portal, but he wants to stop you from entering." Her light extinguished, her body turned to dust, then blew into the wind.

Tracker ran up to Abigail, his white fur turned red. Abigail frantically checked him for wounds, relieved to find the blood wasn't his. She hugged him and rocked him in her arms. He wigged his tailless butt and lifted his lip with a smile. He kissed her on the face. I couldn't hold back. I jumped on him and hugged him, rubbing my scent against his neck. The sun was rising. "Time to go."

THE ROAD TO
DARK CORNER

ABIGAIL FINISHED CLEANING THE BLOOD off Tracker. She picked up Flutter, who was laying on a rock by the water. I paced back and forth along the shore, remembering how Agatha put one foot in front of the other, causing the stepping-stones to rise out of the water. With the morning sun I could see what was swimming under the surface. Like the hellhounds that roamed the woods on the trail to Poinsett Bridge, the water held other demons. Razor-sharp teeth and black soulless-eyed eels unseen to humans, harmless to all but those who walked the trail to the portal. I hadn't told Abigail that for every piece of white magic we picked up along the way a piece of black magic followed us. Newton was right when he said for every action there is an equal and opposite reaction. Time and space are a rubber band, as you stretch it into the future from the present it snaps back into the past the same as magic. The guardians of the trail were waiting to devour not just our flesh but our true light. Tracker growled at them.

"Settle," Abigail said. "You don't want to fight them."

"Step onto the water, Abigail," I told her.

She looked down as one of the creatures raised its head above the water, snapping at us. She glanced at me.

"Believe, Abigail, you have to believe."

She closed her eyes, took a deep breath, and before she could stop herself she stepped out into the water. As she did the first stone rose up to greet her foot. She opened her eyes, balancing herself on the rock as the creatures swam around her, snapping and hissing. She took another step; the next stone rose. I leaped into her arms. Each step she took another stone rose out of the water. Tracker hopped from rock to rock behind us until we reached the far shore. Then the rocks and the creatures disappeared into the deep, cold water.

Abigail took Flutter out of her pocket and raised her hand to the sky. She floated to a bright red hibiscus. And then crisscrossed to an orange one. It was the path from the painting. We followed behind her, marking her way exactly. I could feel the gathering magic around us. We wound our way through the narrow trail, avoiding rocks, holes. We walked this way for miles, following Flutter, swatting at the bees that buzzed around our heads, passing by the North Saluda reservoir until we reached Callahan Mountain Road. The last time I had walked this road it was part of the dirt path of the Asheville Highway. Now it was paved with the occasional car speeding past us. We reached Poinsett Bridge at twilight; all the visitors had left. Or at least the human visitors. I could feel the presence of the others, the ghosts who lingered at the bridge attracted by the energy of the portal, moths to the light.

The humans never ventured here after dark. To them Poinsett Bridge was the most haunted bridge in all of the Carolinas, maybe even the south. We stopped and stared at the bridge, a light fog rising off the stream running through it as the night air cooled off the ground. And then the voices began, some of them crying, others yelling. Apparitions came out of the woods, walking endlessly back and forth over the bridge, their misery dragging behind them like Marley's ghost. At the top of the bridge stood the lieutenant. In his hand he held the head of the young private who tried to warn me at the Biltmore. He tossed the head into the stream. He lifted his sword, and an army of lost souls marched from all sides, surrounding us. Deserters, turncoats, the unforgiven of the war. Abigail clutched her grandmother's amulet around her neck. As she twirled around, a bright light spun in a circle until it became a twister, lifting the undead army into it. Tracker leaped and bit at them, lunging at the ground, twisting and turning trying to grasp flesh that wasn't there. The lieutenant cracked his whip at Tracker, who screamed in pain and fell into the water. I ran to the bridge and clawed my way to the top. I stood on the edge.

"Stop," I cried out.

"Take me into the portal," the lieutenant said. His sword glistened in the moonlight. It was neither a man when I first met him or a ghost when I had seen him last. He was the darkness that had taken the fairies. He smiled his rotting smile. "You understand that I can end you, don't you? Not just this body you're trapped in but your witch's light forever?"

"Take me but spare the girl."

He raised his whip over my head. "Take me to the portal."

I turned as I heard Abigail scream. The soldiers were tearing at her clothes, ripping at her flesh.

A voice called out from under the bridge. "Me save Terra." Pixel charged out from under the arch of the bridge, tearing through the soldiers, swiping his claws, sending them into the mist. He rose up on his hind legs, waving his paws, causing a great explosion. Thousands of pins of light floated down from the trees. I shook my head in disbelief. The fairies flew into battle, waving their wands shooting fairy dust and enclosing the hordes in a great net. Flutter flapped her wings and transformed into a beautiful fairy of the woods, the last fairy of Lullymore. She climbed on top of the dragonfly, and they rode low to the ground as the dragonfly scorched the earth with fire. The lieutenant fell back, holding his arms in front of him as Pixel leaped on top of him, tearing at him. The fairies flew around Pixel. The lieutenant raised his whip once. A lightning bolt crashed across the sky, striking his hand. Mrs. Stickman stood on a hill on the bank of the stream, raising her lightning rod, shooting lightning across the battlefield. Dressed in Viking horns and armor, Mrs. Loblolly sliced through the dead with her broadsword. All the Wiccans battled alongside the fairies.

The lieutenant reached for his whip. Pixel bit his arm. The lieutenant knocked Pixel to the ground. The lieutenant lifted his head off his neck. He raised it in the air. The bridge shook, and black horses pulling a black wagon thundered up the bridge. He climbed up on the wagon. "I call the name Abigail Oakhaven." As he spoke her name, Abigail's body contorted. She lifted off the ground and flew into the wagon, heavy chains wrapped around her.

"Abigail," I shouted over the clash of swords. "Speak it. Speak it now."

Abigail said, "Tied by knots of thread, held by hands of dead, bound by earth, covered by dirt, lie eternal by woods." The horses kicked and reared up, the lieutenant cracked his whip, but it had no power. Its fire was extinguished. The chains broke as Abigail leaped from the wagon. The dead turned to mist and went back into the earth. The lieutenant pulled back on the reins and rode off into the dark.

Pixel stood, shaking himself off. I stared in wonder at him. "Pixel, do good?" he asked.

I tackled him, checking his body, which was healed and strong. "Pixel how?"

"Me friends come. Pixel's army."

Flutter flew down and stood on the stone rim of the bridge. I jumped up next to her, staring into her eyes, such a tiny creature with such a brave heart. She smiled back up at me then looking past me she knelt down. All the fairies joined her, kneeling down next to her. I turned to see who they were bowing to. Behind me stood a young woman with fire red hair, a glimpse of a young Emma Tangledwood. She clasped the ash, oak, and thorn amulet around her neck.

"Charlotte come. Make me better," Pixel said. "Charlotte queen of fairies."

Abigail curtsied to the young girl. Charlotte placed her hands over Abigail's wounds. They healed instantly. Tracker limped up to the bridge. Charlotte knelt down and kissed his head. "Good as new," she said. Tracker ran off, chasing Pixel.

"How did you find us?" Abigail asked.

"My great-aunt came to me in a dream. I've not seen her since I was a little girl. I didn't know she died," Charlotte said. "The dream was so real. I had to come see for myself. She told me to come to the animal hospital where I found Pixel and the ladies of the Biltmore Society. They embraced me in their circle as we prayed for Pixel. I felt a surge of electricity run through them and into me. I felt alive for the first time. All my life I had felt different. At that moment, I knew who I was. I held Pixel in my arms, and he was healed."

Pixel jumped next to Flutter, rubbing his head against her. "Me friend." He giggled.

I glanced down as the bridge shook underneath us. We ran down to the stream. At the end of the tunnel a small vortex of white lights appeared. Instinctively Charlotte walked toward the light, her fairy subjects following her. "Fairies stay," she commanded. She stopped to look back at us with a smile and then she was gone.

Abigail began walking toward the light. "No," I screamed. "Abigail, don't."

"I have to see what's on the other side, Terra." Abigail kept walking.

Elizabeth appeared in the swirl, her arms outstretched, reaching for her great-granddaughter.

"No," I cried, "Abigail, don't."

Pixel wrapped his paws around her leg. She dragged him along the ground. "Abigail, no go."

She reached the portal. Her fingertips touched Elizabeth's. Elizabeth smiled at me, her mouth moving, but no words came out. The roar of the vortex was too loud.

"I can't hear," I screamed above the noise. "Elizabeth, what are you saying?"

Abigail knelt down and hugged me. "I love you, Terra Rowan. I always will." Then she jumped into the portal and it closed after her. Pixel cried. Tracker howled, pacing back and forth where we had last seen her.

EPILOGUE

CONSTRUCTION HAD BEGUN ON THE new Leaf & Page. Only one wall remained from the original building built in 1890. Now Mrs. Twiggs stood back and watched as the bones came together. Carpenters were busy at work, framing out the interior. She walked around inspecting their work, nodding her head. "Looking good, Terra, don't you think?"

I shook my head. She sat on the bench across the street most of the day, watching the old building come to life. As the construction crew finished for the day, we went inside. Albert stood in the corner by the original wall, looking confused and nervous. Mrs. Twiggs reached her hand out. "It'll be as it should be, my love."

"Yes, my love," he replied.

I could see her longing to embrace her beloved, to feel his warmth, to taste his kiss. I struggled but knew what I had to do. After centuries in this body I wanted that moment for myself. Agatha Hollows had gifted me that magic, knowing I would use it at the river to stop the lieutenant, knowing that whatever was left of that magic would give me a moment in my old body. I removed the sliver from my paw. I slowly walked up to Albert and stuck it into his foot. He shook. Mrs. Twiggs stood back. "Terra what have you done?"

She watched as the flesh crawled up from his toes to his legs. He stared at his hands as they became flesh once again, not believing it. He touched his chest, feeling his heartbeat and the warmth of his skin. Before us stood Albert Twiggs, the living. I whispered to Mrs. Twiggs, "It's only for a short time, my dear friend." She grabbed Albert and pulled him close, kissing him passionately. She wrapped her arms around him.

Pixel bounced into the room. He saw them kissing and covered his eyes with his paws. "Terra, we go now."

"Yes, Pixel," I said as we walked into the night. I saw a new twinkle in Pixel's eyes. The fairy dust had turned Pixel. I looked at him. "Pixel, do you want to learn magic?"

"Me magic, Terra?"

"Yes, you."

"Me Terra familiar."

"Not anymore Pixel. You are now a witch's apprentice."

Coming soon: Book 3:

THE WITCHES' APPRENTICE

ABOUT THE AUTHOR

IN THE MIDDLE OF A January snowstorm, Vicki Vass fled her native Chicago and landed an hour outside of Asheville, North Carolina and 30 minutes from Greenville, South Carolina in an area known as the Blue Ridge Escarpment but to locals known as Dark Corner, its history steeped in mystery and magic. While gazing out at the ever-changing Appalachian landscape, she finds inspiration in that history, mystery and lore of the area, which led to the continuing adventures of characters created in Bloodline: A Witch Cat Mystery, Book 1.

An award-winning journalist, Vicki Vass is the author of the Antique Hunters Mystery series. The first book in the series, Murder for Sale, was a finalist for the Mystery & Mayhem award. She has written more than 1,400 articles for the Chicago Tribune as well as other commercial publications including Home & Away, the Lutheran and Woman's World.

She now lives outside of Greenville with her husband, Australian shepherds and the real Terra and Pixel.

BOOKS BY VICKI VASS

Witch Cat Mystery
Bloodline, Book 1
Dark Corner, Book 2

Antique Hunters Mystery Series
Murder for Sale (previously published as Murder by the
Spoonful)
Pickin' Murder
Killer Finds
Key to a Murder
Dressed to Kill

The Postman is Late: Neighborhood Watch Mystery
Gem Hunter: Alex Kustodia Mystery

Science Fiction
Eleven: 1

Made in the USA
Middletown, DE
17 August 2021

46239613R00113